Praise for *The Spark of My Womb*

"This brilliant novel will stick with you long after you finish. *The Spark of My Womb* had a shocking twist I did not see coming, and it's a powerful tribute to the power of women, our resiliency, and our healing. There are only a few books I'd describe as 'life-changing'—and *The Spark of My Womb* is one of them. It will change your heart forever" -Caitlin Elizabeth, Author, Editor

"The kind of book that makes you think, makes you feel, and lets you hope. *The Spark of My* Womb is for all of us. This book will make you think the author has read your journal and then written you a better ending. Delightful. Provocative. A heartfelt homecoming." -Elyse Snipes, MA, LMFT

"*The Spark of my Womb* is a quiet and moving meditation on motherhood, identity, and the mysteries of life itself. Bonnie has crafted a story deeply personal yet universally relatable. Open your mind and enjoy the trip!" -Ethan, Creative Director

"Get ready for a journey that is as fun, insightful, surprising, and maybe even as mind-blowing as a psychedelic trip itself. An artfully crafted and written story that you'll not only totally enjoy, but remember." -Dr. Peggy

"*The Spark of My Womb* is a thrilling and intimate exploration of the human condition. From the opening pages, this book pulls the reader into a narrative that carries a tension and honesty that is so captivating it is hard to put down. It is rare to find a book this fun to read that also helps illuminate my own understanding of self and others. "Jess Martindale, LMFT

"In this beautifully layered novel, B. Coil offers a rare, honest window into the emotional terrain women traverse in the wake of trauma. *The Spark of My Womb* shows that healing is not a straight line but a sacred spiral of memory, connection, and reclamation." -Kyle Horst, PhD., LMFT

"*The Spark of My Womb* is a unique and stunning journey of healing that opened me up to see myself in each of the characters. The writing is brilliant- funny, tender, confronting, and generous. A book that changes something in you comes along once in a while and this is one of those books. I loved it." -Aurora Allen, MA, SEP, RYT-500

"*The Spark of My Womb* is at times both a deeply introspective and poetic exploration of motherhood, grief, and healing, while also reflecting on identity, faith, and resilience. Womb is a text of tethered, woven stories of the human spirit, a dance of grief and rebirth." -Tim S., Professor

"With a single spark, everything can change. In *The Spark of My Womb*, B.Coil ignites a fierce journey through fire, memory, and the alchemy of the psyche - where grief becomes ash, and from that ash, new life blooms. From the suffocating halls of trauma to the fertile depths of the womb, this haunting, lyrical book guides us through the flames of loss and into the light of radical compassion." -Alex M.

The Spark of My Womb

A novel

B. Coil

THE MOONLIGHT GROUP
2025

Published in North America.

Paperback ISBN: 978-1-7342270-8-6

First print edition: 2025

for all the parts of me and the things we couldn't say

Content Warning

This novel contains depictions of emotionally intense and potentially triggering experiences, including pregnancy loss, self-harm, and themes of abandonment. It also touches on childhood trauma, mental illness, and complicated family dynamics. Please take care while reading. Your well-being matters.

1

With one deep breath, I will have a life of my own; burning, destroying, and consuming at whatever rate I see fit. All it takes is one seemingly insignificant spark. A singular element of tiny orange and yellow burning oxidation that will set the whole thing ablaze. I am resourceful. I consume all around me to grow, evolve, bloom, shrink, fade, and eventually die. No one can guess my path, only witness it. Even if I do not know which way the wind will take me, I am free to emerge and dwindle moment by moment. Embers write the pages of my stories, turning core memories and hand-stitched quilts into wayward drifts of black ash. Antiqued baby photos with rounded edges and patch-worked bell bottoms twist and turn under heated duress, fading the life once lived into a pile of cremation. Velvet couches reveal their weakness as they melt quickly, wrapping up the fibers into tiny strips of tar that roll into themselves, allowing the puffy cotton from underneath one more billowing hurrah before it, too, succumbs.

Time stands still as everyone watches. At some point, the police will arrive, then the fire department. Someone must have seen the smoke and called. It was Tom. It's always been Tom. My flames scorch with urgency, the drive to accomplish their mission before being extinguished by the men in yellow. A fire is like a rebirth, a prescribed burn, a thought-out, planned salvation. It is through the destruction that I bring forth a genesis.

The red and blue lights swirl around the night sky, creating a manufactured aurora borealis. I am the goddess of the forest, towering above the trees, my power ascending from the deepest place within me. The ethereal flames are my wings. I am the Siren of the Evergreen, alluring all foliage around me to join in my dance.

The men in yellow pour water on my birthing ceremony. They don't seem to understand that this is not a baptism. They are not the priests, and I am not a poor sinner needing salvation. The crackle of the incineration exceeds the volume of their yelling, turning their screams into whispers.

Just beyond the luminous cloud of my light and heat, bending and swirling as it touches the cool night air, I see a hand touching her shoulder, and a voice calls out her name. Yellow caution tape surrounds the women, blocking them from the rest of the world. This isn't new; isolation has always been a part of their story. The hand on her shoulder tightens, and she reaches to take hold. Her other hand finds the other woman's fingers hanging by her side. Woven together, they stand, my heat giving them the warmth they never received but always longed for. My flames remind them they must never let go, that they can only survive this life with one another. Staring into her eyes, I search until I find the abyss called grief. I rage all around me, getting bigger, fuller, and brighter until I can see the bottom of the chasm and find love. I see babies and families, dreams and despairs; all encapsulated within the most messianic part of her body. Her womb space.

2
London

Filling out the mental health questionnaire feels a lot like staring into a gene pool of doom. The family history glares back at me like a red flag warning: breast cancer for all the women on both sides, but also optimistic things like (but not limited to) lung cancer, cervical cancer, and high blood pressure. They seem to think we can change our genetics with diet and positive thinking. But changing our brains? I am still skeptical. This, I guess, is why I am here and enrolled in this study.

I look at the study questionnaire with a sense of dread. *Is it possible to be too messed up to be qualified?* If I am honest, I am drowning. I heard a talk once about how the average person blinks 13,000-16,000 times a day and that because of this, we are a species accustomed to living with light and darkness. The point, this man said, was to assess how you view your life: is it a long corridor of dark with light dispersed throughout, or is it a hall of miracles with a few dark days? This talk was supposed to inspire me, but it only confirmed what I already knew to be true: I am a pessimist but with good reason. I come by the dark hall honestly.

The first page is accessible, and I get through it quickly: age, height, last menstrual cycle, and any current ailments or allergies. But as soon as I turn it over, my breath catches in my chest.

Do you have any past unresolved traumas?

The title of my memoir will be precisely that. I have been in and out of therapy so much, with so many diagnoses and medications, that I honestly can't remember which issues have been resolved and which ones still linger, haunting me when they decide the time is right. Which, I have learned, is never the right time. But since these are *psychedelic drugs* we are talking about here, I decided to list all the ones that I can remember:

> My mother died when I was 6
> My house burned down the summer before 7th grade
> I had a stillborn baby when I was in my late twenties
> etc.

People probably don't write "etc." when they list their traumas, but I'm not sure how to denote that these are the *primary* traumas. Because of these ones, I have a few, smaller, what I would call *secondary* traumas. I can always explain things in my interviews, I guess.

The trial is for those who have post-traumatic stress disorder. While that has only been one of my many diagnoses over the years (anxiety, depression, bipolar *maybe*, and borderline personality disorder), my therapist seemed to think it was the root issue that caused all the others. *The domino effect* was her exact words. Line them up and knock them down.

The whole process consists of this questionnaire, an interview over Zoom, and then a psilocybin trip at Pacific Coast

Medical Institute, which should take one full day of work between check-in and post-integration. I will also get paid $600. Next question.

Can you pinpoint what your primary triggers are?

If I write "everything," will they think it's hyperbole? I wish that I were kidding, but my anxiety has gotten so bad that I have hardly left the house. Everything reminds me of everything else, and I find myself assigning meaning where it doesn't belong. I write narratives about things that haven't happened yet, things that most likely won't happen, and then I freeze. I simply write "N/A."

What medications are you currently taking?

I ran out of the prescriptions that didn't seem to help, but I have stuck with Xanax for quite some time. Over the years, I have been given lithium, Lexapro, gabapentin, and a few others I can't quite remember. Some had suicidal ideation warnings, so the next question is tricky for me to answer.

Have you ever thought about harming yourself?

At first, I write, *I mean, who hasn't?* But then I erase it against my better judgment. The truth is, I have thought about ending the noise in my head so many times. When nothing seems to work, and I keep getting sent to different therapists who all have the next drug for me to try, but the effects are only temporary, I begin to see a common denominator: *me.* So yes, I have thought about harming myself, but no, I have never made plans to do so. That is what I write, and I hope it's enough.

The final question, like me, is all twisted in knots.

> *If you could be free from all your triggers,*
> *what would you do with your life?*

I can not fathom a life without my triggers. I can not imagine an existence where I do not have to cater to my traumas. I close my eyes and think about my life: from the outside, it is boring and mundane, but I live in the deep waters of fear, shame, and darkness. Everything is enormous, and I long for it to be boring. I wish for my mind to be so blank that I could do something for fun. Go on a walk just to hear the birds sing. I never could watch the waves crash without wondering what lurks beneath or how I might want to surf. I imagine a day I am *free*, free from obligations, worry, stress, pills, mantras, meditations, manifesting, or anything else I have tried that never works.

I would paint.

3
Peggy

I have a concise amount of time to earn her trust. It's a crucial element, maybe the most important one in being a Guide. The journey will be full of wild terrains, intimate meetings, ups and downs. It is tumultuous and sometimes beautiful but sometimes terrifying and exhilarating. Psilocybin is disarming, a dissolving of boundaries and ego, an unfamiliar and uncomfortable place for most. If, in the middle of it, she feels like she may die, it is me she must trust to see her out of it.

I have been an Expert Guide with Pacific Coast Medical Institute for over thirty years. Brought on to conduct studies of psilocybin before we knew its full power, I have seen its use and popularity rise along with its necessity. I'll never forget going to an old friend's house for dinner, bringing the wine and the flowers, sitting on his back porch amidst his garden, thinking we were just two friends spending time together. And we were.

He and I met during a meditation practice, as much as you can meet someone while meditating. In my first years of practicing Buddhism, I entered the Sangha, adorned my robe, sat down to meditate, hung up my robe, and left. The first years of practice called for this individualism. I needed the time and space to have an internal experience before letting others in. I didn't know the Self at all. I knew my ego but not the Self. But over time, I needed the opposite: the unity that being together offers. I finally began seeing myself when I went to events like Cookies and Koans or met for picnics and weekend retreats. Only when I learned the path and pain of others deeply enough did I learn to accept the path and pain inside myself.

He was one of my first connections. I spilled his teacup at my first social at the sangha, and where I thought this would rule me out of the conversation, it invited me to begin. Like me, he had come from a more fundamental Protestant background, and after a life full of the duality and twists and turns it offers, we had found ourselves right here. Over time, we became dear friends, and our friendship blossomed over dinners, walks, and coffee shops. A medical doctor by trade, I have deep respect for the work he does in the world. He once told me that he has about twenty minutes to earn the trust of his patients, an intuitive art that he has since taught me all about. But he loved medicine and kept what he was working on private for the most part. I knew he was contemplating leaving his private practice to start a job with PCMI, so I assumed we would be celebrating that night.

I was only half-correct. He was accepting a job at this highly esteemed university, the Pacific Coast Medical Institute, known for its out-of-the-box thinking in the psychiatric field. But I didn't see his offer coming that evening; he wanted me to accompany him. PCMI was starting a center for psilocybin, and he wanted me, of all people, to become an "Expert Guide," as he called it. They had given him full reign over the whole program, and hiring me was his first order of business. I was flattered, of course, but completely unprepared. A librarian by day and a wine and TV dinner kind of gal by night, I had never worked in the medical or mental health field before. But I did what my Buddhist practice taught me to do. I sat with the invitation and asked myself, "Is this right for me?"

And here I am, thirty years later, thousands of patients later, contemplating if my time with PCMI is over. Don't get me wrong, I have loved my time here, but as I sit and wait for my next client to arrive, the nagging feeling that something is missing tugs at my core yet again. When I first started doing psilocybin trials, we had a freedom that we absolutely took for granted. It was a new drug, and the facilitation was all sort of up in the air. We learned a lot as we went. We got into situations where we didn't know what to do, but we let our intuition lead the way. We made playlists and discovered the perfect type of setting. We took our time, and our clients did, too. It was blissful, the facilitating of journeys almost like taking the drug itself. I was on a high for every trip, even when they didn't go as planned. Sometimes, people didn't have the experience they were hoping for—and neither did we. But we learned that every journey was what each person needed to move forward. Sometimes, it was a meeting of the psyche; others, it was tough love from those they met while on the journey; and still others, it was the disappointment that nothing occurred. Those early days were marked by courage and risk, trial and error, dosing, and new research.

Now, it's still good. But it's also structured and formulated. Everything is set, and most of my job is teaching others how to do it. How do you teach that which should be innate? Many of those who want to be Guides come because of their own experience and are usually disarmed enough to begin unlearning everything we teach them until they can find their own music within the manuals. My favorite part is finding myself and the tune I dance to with my clients. And yet. I've been doing this for decades. I know I am not done yet, but I might be with this iteration. I can feel something new growing, but I can't quite grasp exactly what. Working for an institution means my waking and best hours are spent within the system, a necessary evil for an illegal and politically charged drug that has lots of red tape around it. And so, I prepare for another client, hoping this one may unlock something new inside me.

***

She enters the room slowly and sees me sitting on the couch in a white medical coat from across the room. *Trust begins now.* I stand up, approaching her slowly. Having read her chart, I know a little of what she has been through. I smile and introduce myself, and she replies, "Nice to meet you. I'm London."

What happens next is a delicate dance that is much more like learning to be a midwife than a mechanic. Over the three decades of my work as a Guide, I have learned that I must live in a world of paradox. I know and memorize the playbook, but also, know when to throw it all out the window. I listen to her story, empathize and understand, and never stand in judgment. My most significant task is to do nothing at all.

"London. I'm so glad you're here. Let's sit together." I motion for her to sit on the couch, offering her a blanket if needed.

My Buddhist background offers me the training to be present. I first learned to be present in my own life enough to understand my shortcomings, my delusions, and my worth *with* them and not against them. The voices inside of me must be heard if I want to understand them. The more I work on myself, the more I can work with whoever walks through the door.

Since PCMI is a medical facility, it is a more sterile environment than I would ideally like; the only decor consists of a table in the corner with a small candle, a tiny painting of the "Tree of life", a glass of water, and a feather I use for sensation purposes when a client is having trouble transitioning down from the medicine. I also snuck in a few colorful pillows and two blankets, which I pack in and out after each session. Otherwise, my presence must be the warmth in the cold and minimalistic room; it is the only gift I can offer—a deep and abiding presence alongside someone as they unpack their trauma.

"London, I've read your chart, but I'd like to hear from you. What brings you here today?" I maintain a relaxed posture but always keep eye contact. I wait for her answer as long as it takes her to give it. I can not force it. The number one rule is that if trust isn't built, we do not proceed.

"I do things and think things that I don't like doing, but I do not know how to stop doing or thinking about them." She looks away from me as if I will see and know exactly what she is talking about.

"I understand. I do and think things I do not like doing, either," I tell her. She looks up at me, surprised.

"You do?" she asks, her eyes wide and innocent.

"How do you think I got into this work? Because I needed it myself." I pull the blanket over my lap and pour a cup of hot tea.

"What's going to happen? What is it like?" She mimics me. Her shoes come off, and she pulls her knees up to her chest, covering everything but her head and neck in the blanket.

"It depends," I say, a matter of fact.

"On what?" she asks, and I can see her mental wheels turning, wondering if she's done the right thing or enough to prepare.

"On whatever is going on in your body. Your mind. Plant medicine works with what is already going on inside you. We know from scientific studies that psilocybin specifically works with what is the SH2A receptor in our brains. It promotes a sort of interconnectivity in which our brain communicates with its multiple parts in a way that it doesn't normally do. So whatever exists in those neuropathways, whatever parts of your brain have become isolated from others, the psilocybin will connect the dots."

This is my most scientific and truthful answer. Psilocybin has an intuitive nature about it, and no person's experience is like another's. I've been with people who have had a life-changing journeys; something has been altered in these clients so profoundly that the integration happens independently. In others, the journey serves as something with potential. It creates a memory that can be picked apart, analyzed, and studied.

"But on a more practical note, you and I will get to know each other over the next hour. If, and only if, you are ready, we will proceed. At that time, if you decide you are ready to take the Psilocybin, I will be with you throughout the whole process. You may or may not be able to hear me unless you ask for me, but mostly I will keep quiet. I let your brain sort out what it needs to do independently. How does that sound?" I take a sip of my tea and repeat a mantra in my head that I always do at this stage in the game: "*I have everything I need.*"

The best gift I can give London is my quiet presence. If I talk too much during her experience, I force her to work against plant medicine. Activating the speaking centers of the brain is to fight against the unfolding. I am not here to fix anything; I am here to birth what is already inside of her.

She yawns, a sign that her nervous system has come down from whatever state she came here with. She's ready to meet me, and I am here. And so I sit and wait, a push and pull of infinity symbols until she feels safe and secure enough to proceed.

4
Amy

Phew! It turns out I don't want to commit suicide; I just want to visit London.

The thought feels like a balm to my racing, anxious mind. The hamster stops running on the wheel. My eyes fly open as soon as I have this epiphany, and I quickly stop the meditation on my smartphone app. *It isn't quite finished, but close enough.* Frantically, my fingers move as if time is running out. I search for flights and a hotel before the idea escapes me. The adrenaline rush of a new adventure, or maybe a distraction, surges through my caffeinated veins. I can see it in my shaky fingers as they tremble enough to make the search more difficult. My heart rate slightly elevates. Reality tries to poke at the corner of my mind in the form of my husband's schedule or the printed off-school calendar that hangs tauntingly on my fridge only a few steps away. *I will cross that bridge once a flight is secured.*

I have never been to London. I have never even been to Europe. My days are spent racing around the bumper-to-bumper freeways of Orange County, chauffeuring kids around, doling out organic snacks on the way to soccer practice; keeping up with the Joneses (the actual names of our neighbors) and all the other PTA moms who have worked their whole lives to live here in Newport Beach and send out the Christmas card with the address prominently placed in cause anyone on the list might not already know of the prestigious zip code. This European adventure, this breakthrough, is more of a calling. My therapist, Lyz (pronounced "*LYZ*" with an air of emphasized annoyance), says that escaping is a defense mechanism and that Instagram pictures of Big Ben, coffee shops, and the West End won't solve my chronic, sometimes debilitating, anxiety that centers around my lack of self-worth. (Lyz's opinion; not necessarily my own.) But Lyz also says, like my husband, that perhaps I need a break from my life—a little reprieve. "Not sustainable" is what Lyz, the Therapist, called my day-to-day. And yet.

How am I supposed to leave? I run this house. I do every small and big thing that keeps everyone alive and happy. I carry all the baggage of my emotions and everyone else who walks through the door, sits at the dinner table, and cries or complains about their "boring" life. If someone is upset because someone at school was rude? They take it out on me—the Mom. If someone didn't sleep enough, they lost at Monopoly because their brother bought Boardwalk, or maybe they don't like to do chores—it is my fault for ruining their lives. If half of the things said to me were told to my mother growing up, I would have been thrown over my father's knee so fast and been spanked right on my ass. Spanking was the parenting tool of the 90's. But now, professionals have researched children's emotions and how to be attuned to your kids and shit. It's such hard work. Parenting, before kids, didn't seem like it was so *involved.*

Lyz also says I need better emotional and energetic boundaries, which may be accurate, but is this possible as a mother? It goes against a primal instinct that gets ignited when mothers see their brood hurting. A switch turns on, and a fire begins to burn deep in the pit of a mother's stomach. Her whole body responds, and she goes into action mode. She problem-solves, and she and her kin talk it out, and she will have a meditation, a snack, or a cup of tea ready. A mother helps her young come down from daily stressors, and she feels, once again, after a day of laundry, grocery shopping, and wiping down countertops and windows, that she has a purpose. But, as my children return to a calm state, my whole being stays activated. I can't come down the same way I teach my children to do. And the fire burns and burns, making its way up from the pit of my stomach to my forehead, and a headache begins, and when it's there, it's hard for me to return to myself. Again, this is Lyz's "professional opinion".

But, like, what does Lyz know? I have seen Lyz for over two years and have done everything she said. I have exhausted the list. I am a perfect patient, so the fact that my anxiety or low self-esteem is still hanging around isn't exactly my fault. To quote Lizzo, I *did the damn work, and it didn't work.* What if it *is* London? What if escaping is the exact thing I need? Would Lyz reimburse me for the countless money spent on therapy? Or maybe I invoice Lyz for the cost of the trip?

My search brings up the cutest town that is everything I imagine the UK countryside to be: bright, lush meadows for days, cobblestone streets, and houses with porches that boast a view that I know will make me stay in the same spot the whole day. Plus, there's a castle with a garden and some nearby pubs, and the trip time to London isn't awful. I close my eyes and picture myself there. I am still. I am calm. I am quiet. I am making pizza by hand from the local farmers market in London because I hear my gluten intolerance is different in Europe. The anxiety doesn't follow me to London. With a deep sigh, I open up a new tab and am about to search for flights until I remember the dreadful reality that I don't have a passport. *Fuuuuuck.* I know I need a passport for "emergency use," but that's for apocalyptic-level, oh-no-he-got-re-elected scenarios, not needing to escape from one's regular life. No one prepares a Mom for that. The thought of figuring out the paperwork is overwhelming. Paperwork is for adults, and I have always felt that giving birth was more accessible than filling out the paperwork that followed. Contractions over documents every damn day. Throwing my phone in defeat towards the end of the couch, I sense my idea fading into the background as I slip back into the mundane.

The morning routine has become complicated and arduous. My children long for independence, so they revolt at everything I suggest, but they still aren't independent enough to make a sandwich. My friends, family, and random voices on the internet claim that I will miss these mornings someday. All the making of sandwiches, fruits, veggies, and chips crammed into a lunch that they won't eat must be relished because, one day, every Mom will wake up when she wants to, and she will have no one to make lunch for, and she will be devastated by this reality.

This does not compute.

Who has ever had twenty-five years of being yanked out of bed and into a kitchen and chauffeur job that never pays—and doesn't hope for the day that it ends? And yet, the quiet that greets me now when I return home from the morning madness makes me feel alone, afraid, and completely worthless. I am the only one that is not out in the world. I don't have anyone to answer to—I make little to zero income. I am the one who chose this life, feels trapped by it, but can't leave it behind. I take more than I give. I am a waste of space.

I can't pinpoint when this feeling began or how fast it took over, but considering the timeline of events, I am pretty sure it had grown at the same rate as my ever-expanding thighs and lower belly I never had before. This was my go-to marker for trying to control my life: how much I weighed and how big I looked. This crept slowly up on me as I approached 40, and just one morning, the jeans I always wore stopped fitting. And they haven't fit since. They get stuck halfway up my hips, and nothing zips, buttons, or budges. I keep returning to these denim atrocities, and the same thing happens every time: I berate myself about how fat I am, take them off, put on my sweatpants, and either eat chocolate or pour a glass of wine. It depends on the time of day, of course. Lyz says to stop trying the jeans on, but what can I say? I've grown accustomed to this little self-berating ritual.

The daily denim ceremony reminds me of the assignment from my well-meaning (and highly qualified) therapist to keep track of my self-talk. Lyz said I must journal what my inner voice is telling me. With a sigh, I pop back into the notes app on my phone, noticing for a moment the sound my acrylic nails make on the screen, and with great satisfaction, I realize that I did, in fact, already complete today's assignment. *Amy: 1, Lyz: 0.* But it doesn't matter, really; I could copy and paste the journal entry of each day until eternity because every day, the same thoughts run through my head as I stumble my way into the bathroom:

1. You are fat and lazy. You're fat because you are lazy.
2. You have no talents
3. You are a fool
4. Your dreams are ridiculous
5. Should I google what is wrong with _______

It's only 6:04 am.

Defeated but committed to the defeat, I get up to refill my coffee, slower than I'd like; residual back pain from an injury six years ago. Another appointment option looms in my head; maybe a dose of physical therapy could fill my time, but the thought leaves before it becomes a to-do list. *I'd have to make small talk.*

As I shuffle unevenly back to the coffee maker, the ongoing reminder of pain spirals from my body to my mind and back to my body. It's overwhelming. As I refill my cup, watching the steam billow up from the hot brown cup of courage, I immediately decide to quit my therapist. *Bye LYZ! LYZ* (spelled with a "y" for reasons she won't reveal to me no matter my prodding) is friendly and kind, and indeed, she has been successful with all of her other clients, but it is clear that I am the exception to the rule. This isn't Lyz's fault entirely. It's because I am an Enneagram 4, which qualifies me as a unique flower/rainbow of a human, who no one, not even doctorate-level Lyz, can pin down.

Sure, Lyz's expertise has helped quell the fear that kept me and the kids imprisoned in our own home. Despite a few panic attacks, I managed to survive a global pandemic. It gave me a sense of unrequited recognition that germs *are* everywhere and that we should all be slightly afraid. Sure (see #5 on the list), I still struggle with "fixating" (Lyz's words) when a child has a small scratch, and I find myself googling "flesh-eating bacteria" for hours on end like some person with an addiction. But for the most part, I am much better. It is a damning feeling to overcome a considerable obstacle only to find one buried underneath. The proverbial mental health iceberg that no one ever said was coming. My experience of being human is like an onion: peeling away the layers and crying the whole time.

But when I write, I never cry. The fictional characters and their details give me an excuse to research and obsess over their character's made-up ailments and problems, and then I project less on my kids. Manifesting and burning sage throughout the house was a logical next step because I needed discipline and routine to feel safe and keep my goal of finishing my first book. While sometimes these practices slipped into OCD, they mostly kept me on track with my writing, and for a whole year, when I wrote that book, I felt almost normal again.

And then, I finished the book. The manifesting went into overdrive, but nothing but rejection letters poured in. And in. And in. An unpublished novel sits on my computer screen, the cursor no longer blinking, and the longer it sits, the faster the negative self-talk comes back, then the anxiety, and then my thighs begin to chafe in the Texas heat. This is what Lyz calls "a spiral."

I grab my phone again and turn to my favorite friend and foe, Google Search. Is there a therapy that does not involve digging up every trauma and then thinking about it for an hour at a time, after which I must go back into my life as usual? Deep down, I know what I need: a paid-for London vacation in which I clear my aura, become whole, and eat all the gluten.

A text message comes through, interrupting my determination. It's only 6:20 a.m. *Who in the world?* It's Isla from the book club reminding the group of the next book, Michael Pollan's *How to Change Your Mind*. I have had a month to read it, but of course, I have not found the time. I *have* the time, but when you're depressed, time stands still and also becomes wholly lost.

A quick Amazon search reveals that Pollan wrote a book about medicinal mushrooms—psychedelics. I buy it. It will arrive exactly two days before book club, giving me two days to get lost in the read and, hopefully, two days without my anxious racing mind or deep hollow feeling inside. "Loving this book! Can't wait to discuss!" I type back. White lies keep me accountable.

No one in the house is awake yet. The stillness is unwelcome. I can hear my thoughts beginning to whisper in the back of my mind, the ones I so readily push down. Instead, I open up Instagram. And like the gods are in charge of the algorithm, a face from the past, a woman I knew who became a therapist, shows up first in my feed. She looks blissful. Her pores are non-existent. Her eyes are closed, and a small smile spreads across her face. The mountains behind her are massive, with white peaks, and her caption reads: " Mushrooms are not just for pizza. #Psychadelics #trip #expansion #experiemntaltherpay". I slide into her DMs.

"Hey! Long time no talk. I just saw your recent post, and I'd love to know more about your experience with medicinal mushrooms. I'm at a bit of a crossroads, and I could use something new to light the fire again if you will. Hope you're doing well!"

A new anxiety rears its head again. Can a person get caught on drug charges for talking about this? Shit. Phone vibrates.

"Hey! I was thinking about you! [I doubt that] *I can pass along the number of the psychiatrist who led me through my experience. It was amazing. I had a huge creative unlock! I highly recommend it. Here is her email: drlauren@me.com"*

Ook. A psychiatrist. It's probably safe, right? A quick Google search revealed that she is only a day trip away from me and is taking inquiries with a referral.

"Awesome! Thank you! Would you mind referring me? Her website says she only takes referrals. I don't want to put you out, so it's okay if you can't. ;)"

A smiley wink? What the hell? I roll my eyes at myself. Why am I always so awkward?

"Yes, I'll send an email right now. Just wait five minutes and then send yours. You'll love her; she is an excellent guide. She is intuitive, safe, and walks you through the process."

"Awesome! I can't wait! This feels like a real Universe moment because I was just about to read Pollan's new book! Wow!!! Is there anything else you want to tell me about her?"

The exclamation marks make me look like an over-enthusiastic psychopath, but by using my finger to cover them up, it's clear I sound like a serial killer without them. Taking a deep breath (thank you, meditation app), I try, yet again, to loosen the tightness of my shoulders that has been there for about a decade. Closing my eyes, I imagine myself up north, the crisp air, the expansive sky, and I breathe for real, for the first time all morning. It is not London, but maybe it's better. Perhaps I could write a bestseller if this psychedelic trip gives me a creative breakthrough. No, a Pulitzer winner. And then I wouldn't have to *visit* London; I could have my *second home* in London.

Typing up an email to Dr. Lauren, I feel hopeful for the first time in a long time. A sense of superiority creeps in; I've only needed a guide. It's not my fault I am the way I am; maybe I don't need to do anything more than just be set free. The phone buzzes. It's an Instagram notification.

"Yeah, but….you'll see when you get there."

B. COIL

5
Jane

The morning sickness wakes me before my alarm clock. Hot sweats followed by a fierce desire to vomit, I rush to the toilet, opening the lid with my right hand and my left clumsily holding back my hair into a makeshift ponytail. I haven't been getting much sleep, and I can't remember when I have ever been more tired in my entire life. The mornings are the worst, and it seems to wear off as the day progresses. But, since I am the manager, I work a full-day shift, and thus, I switched my shift to afternoons and evenings to avoid puking on the job. I have worked at the same place for five years. I love and hate my job, something my dad warned would happen no matter what I did for a living.

The tile on the bathroom floor is cold and feels soothing to my cheek as I lie down on it, waiting for the dizziness to pass. I have never been good with being sick. Since my mom passed, it was my dad who had to comfort me and care for me if I was ill, and his motherly instincts were about as good as mine. Childish and wishing she was there. How would I raise this baby if I didn't have a mom of my own? I have no example of a mother to follow, no grandmas I've met, no living aunts or even teachers who took me under their wing. My dad did his best, but he was a farmer through and through. I was mostly left to figure stuff out on my own, and when I got my first period, it was my best friend Grace who told me what to do with a tampon. The thought of this brings me a smile, and I slurp up the drool falling out of my mouth and wipe it with my hand. Slowly, I get back on my feet and head into the kitchen to make coffee. I read online that women who are pregnant shouldn't drink coffee in their first trimester, but I tried this for a few days, and the headache was so bad I couldn't get out of bed. Since I haven't seen a doctor yet, I will plead the 5th until they tell me otherwise.

With the hot mug, I settle gently into my blue leather couch. The color of the sky, this purchase was simultaneously absolutely unnecessary and utterly essential. It was way more than I could afford. Still, the day Daddy and I saw it at the store, we both immediately sat down in it, put our feet up on the store coffee table (old habits die hard), and sat in its embrace, enjoying the luxury of it until the store owner told us they were closing. We left imprints where our bodies sat. I pushed it out of my mind when I walked out that door because I was a farm girl leaving the farm to work as a manager at the fancy grocery store in a small but touristy town-just like a good ol' Dixie Chicks song. Unless I was getting royalties from the times I played my favorite country tracks; there was no way I could afford that couch.

But Daddy found a way, and he always does. The day I moved into my apartment, he surprised me with it, rolling it right off the truck with a big ol' smile on his face like it was the best thing he had ever done for me. But that's how Daddy always was: a sucker for big gestures, for pieces of furniture or dishes you'd have for a lifetime. "It matches your eyes, Janey," he said as he ripped off the cellophane wrapping. I was his blue-eyed girl. My heart sinks thinking about how he always thinks the best of me but has no idea that I am now knocked up. At least I didn't conceive her on the couch. I said "*her*."

I shift uncomfortably, my thighs sticking to the leather. The coffee tastes delicious. I bought the beans with my discount at the store and the creamer from Jake's dairy farm. He saves me a bottle of cream off the top, the best part of the milk, which I remember from milking Daisy. After Mama died, we stopped milking cows for a while and then owning cows altogether. Mama loved her cows like she loved me, and I think it was easier for Daddy to pretend they were never there than for him to continue the legacy. We each dealt with her death in our own ways, but those ways never included talking about it. He was a simple countryman with few words. We didn't have a funeral for her. "Your mother wouldn't want all that fuss," he said. And to this day, I don't know the exact details of how she died. There was an accident in the middle of the night, and when I woke up the following day, she was gone. Daddy said he would tell me when I was older, but I didn't want to know as I got older. My imagination has always been one of my favorite things about me, but in this case, I thought it would serve me wrong. My picture of Mama is her tucking me into bed at night; she and I milking Daisy the cow; eating fresh bread and cinnamon rolls; learning to sew; and reading books under the blankets. Whatever horrific thing happened to her that night, I don't want the picture inserted between the beautiful memories that I hold of her. So, I left it at that and have never looked back.

Every Sunday while growing up, my dad and I milked our cow, who was never named. Naming animals was not a practice on the farm for apparent reasons. But when I was 5, they got a new cow that I fell in love with. My mother saw the look of kinship in my eyes, and we made a silent pact and named the beloved cow "Daisy." Together, out in the fields or the milking parlor, we whispered *Daisy* in the cow's ear any chance we had. *Daisy. Daisy.* I was so young then, but this memory has been a solid anchor. After my mom died, I began finding wild, picked daisies outside on the windowsill of my bedroom for me to find. I never asked my dad outright because who else would it be? It was how my mother lived inside of me, an attempt by my father to remind me that mom was always with us. He was a rugged, overall-wearing, beard-growing farmer who loved childhood magic. Year after year, I collected and held on to the daisies, pressing them between the pages of my favorite books, preserving their memory. Some girls had pictures of their mothers; I had dried daisies.

My dad and I never went to church. My parents weren't religious on account of growing up religious, so they ditched it as soon as they could. My mom was raised Christian, and my dad was Catholic, but I didn't learn much about either of these religious institutions until I was much older and people began inviting me to church with them on Sundays. While at first, it felt good to be included, it didn't take long to decipher it was a pity invite: the poor farm girl whose mother had died, and, based on the rules of their religion, most of the town assumed mama went to hell. The invites to sleepovers, where I fell asleep and woke up first because I was on farm time, were a feeble attempt to get her father to say yes to a church invite in the morning. Friends who pitied me were not real friends, and I knew that, but it gave me a chance to forget the deep grief that made a home inside of me for a brief moment. The girls' houses smelled of fresh flowers, the carpets were always vacuumed, and the decorations matched and were updated occasionally. My house stayed the same. Death had sent Dad into a time warp, unable to move forward, unable to relish in the past. He stood smack dab in the middle of suspended time like a second hand on a clock still ticking but going nowhere. *Tick. Tick. Tick.* Chores and sunsets marked the days. My hair grew, and the school grades passed. All boxes on a calendar that could be marked or celebrated. But his mind stood still. *Tick. Tick. Tick.* He was jittery those years after Mama died. His wife. He was often caught off guard by a sound or a car on the dirt driveway, and a flash of hope came across his face as if he had expected her to return.

But before trying to be saved by the well-meaning mothers in town, mama said milking the cow was better than a church. Daisy never judged them for getting out there late; she let them talk while they did their work and freely gave everything that belonged to her. Mama said this is why nature was her God: it did what the other religions only said they would do. Mama often brought her coffee and squirted the fresh milk straight into the mug. Daisy loved being milked. When her teets were full, she slowly approached in pain. They were bulging, and the veins popped out of her. Mama said her breasts got big like that when she was nursing, too. I was so young then that the ancestral metaphor found in the primal action of milking Daisy alongside my mama was lost on me.

My phone chimes, and a text message comes from work. My co-manager (and friend) Sally wants to know if I want the day off because the store is overstaffed. "Yes, please!!" I write over-enthusiastically, and three smiling emojis are sent back. I met Sally at the shop, and we hit it off almost immediately. She is my age, kind, funny, and from the city. I love hearing her stories of taking the subway to school, seeing grass for the first time in a park, and how she doesn't miss it. Sally knows everything about me; she is the only friend I've made and held on to as an adult, but I haven't told her yet that I am pregnant.

I am not sure I will. Because I am not confident, I will keep her. *Her.*

I take another sip of my coffee and close my eyes, recalling all too well what all the church-goers in my hometown would say about an abortion. Burned into my mind are the poster boards with a wooden stick attached tucked away in their garages, ready for use at any moment. I shudder. Hate requires so much effort, I don't think I'll ever understand it.   And yet. What would it be like to know what to do? Even if you didn't quite comprehend it or even really agree, you could consult a book that told you the right answers. As much hate as I saw the church spew, I couldn't help but feel jealous of the assurance that came with it all.

This thought creates a deep sadness, traveling from my mind into my tear ducts and, finally, settling in my chest. I begin to cry in a way that seems to be a new and ongoing occurrence now. I've never been a crier before. I was a farm girl. I rubbed some dirt on it and moved on. But I can't stop these tears. It is an ugly cry that involves my entire body shaking and small lurches forward. I feel the insides of me ripping apart, bleeding decades' worth of aches and grief that I have held in all this time. My nose is running uncontrollably, and I feel the urge to throw up again. This time, from pain, grief, and longing, as if it is begging to get out. Rushing to the bathroom, I collapse beside the toilet, my elbows resting on the seat, staring straight into the white porcelain that gives way to the dark emptiness of the drain—covered in cold sweats, a guttural yell comes from my mouth, a calling out for the voice I need to tell me what to do. The one I need to comfort and hold me. I scream and bang my fists against the wall, calling out her name in desperation that maybe she would come forth and save me like God saved all the people in my town. "MOMMMMMMM!" I yell at the top of my lungs, causing my whole stomach to lurch, and I throw up everything that is, somehow, still inside me.

B. COIL

6
Dr. Lauren

In the sun, every cell rises to the top of my skin barrier, determined to soak in the Vitamin D. The chirp of my email chimes loudly, interrupting my thoughts as I sit in my favorite Adirondack chair on the wooden porch. *Damn. I forgot to put it on silent.* It's rare that I accidentally let in the outside world. A chime isn't just a chime; it is an interruption in my carefully curated bubble of peace. The truth is, I need to see clients because they pay for my food and the roof over my head, but that is all they are: a means to an end. Simply a way to survive. I am only responsible for myself and, of course, Theo. My grumpy, gray cat who wandered in here years ago, and we've formed a routine together. But if times get rough, even Theo would abandon ship. I can tell he is not a "till death do us part" type of cat.

In recent months, the seasons changed and life outside this little A-frame treehouse kept on living and the colors morphed from greens to oranges to bare and then blooms and pollinators, and it became increasingly clear to me that my life's purpose was lost-to put it mildly. My hermit-based existence was, at first, a cold spring on a hot day. At first, it was the healing balm I needed to soothe the fresh wounds of the past, but now it felt more like a prison sentence, a punishment I gave myself. As much as I hated it, I knew I would never stop. Letting the outside world in meant I would need to face the pain of why I was the way I was in the first place. And that is something I was sure I could not endure. I could feel myself pulling inward more and more each day, and now, I only read and answer emails once a week. If my clients need to see me so desperately, they can wait.

And they do. My waitlist is two years long.

At first, I only had a handful of people inquire about my retreats. Since what I do is an anomaly, I was able to charge a high price, thus allowing for only a handful a year. Lately, the chiming of the inbox has been frequent. When I remember to keep my notifications silenced, I return to dozens upon dozens of inquiries daily—the *irony of posting your self-healing for the world to see* as I roll my eyes in disgust. I turn down most requests that come in. I wrote the questionnaire required by potential clients to weed out the problematic and frankly annoying people to work with: lazy, entitled people who expected a specific outcome from their retreat. And, I never accept anyone I might know, even if it was by the 6th degree. I have administered psychedelics long enough to know they were not the end-all solution that everyone hoped for. I didn't want to be stuck with someone who spent the whole time blaming me for their problems not being solved during our three days of integrative therapy post-psychedelic trip. I learned that the hard way.

I close my eyes and tilt my head toward the sun, allowing its beams to be the spotlight on my mind's eye, and I try to imagine Amy, the most recent inquiry, with me in my house, tucked back in these woods. I love my little treehouse, built on the side of the mountain, with one large trunk that goes through the center of the living room. When I found it, it was a total shack, it looked like a horror movie house where at least ten people were murdered, and then they all came back to haunt it, thus the basis of its appeal. I've always loved a good ghost story- a haunting. Spirits with unfinished business are my exact type of company. It's proof that I am not alone, that others have lived with wounds so deep that they couldn't heal them while they were alive. I need a mug that reads "future ghost."

Amy's picture makes me smile. There is something about her that is warm and disarming. In the age of the Instagram filter, I find it endearing that she sent in a photo taken at an unflattering angle, with food that has spilled on her shirt (a hamburger maybe?), her mouth wide open in laughter. I look into her cheerful eyes, wide grin, and well-defined dimples, and at the exact time that I feel the corner of my lips turn up into a smile, my gut twists and turns like a gut punch. A deep pain sears through my solar plexus and travels up until it gets tangled into a knot in my throat, and I begin to cry.

I can't remember the last time I laughed. Not alone. Not with other humans. Not with Theo. I never talk about anything funny with clients. It's all ceremony and ritual and tears and trauma. Everyone enters the door like they are walking through a threshold, their faces solemn, their steps unsure. I feel the energy they bring into the room; some feel like they are in a straight jacket. Others begin the walk up to the house undimmed, excited almost. I watch them as they park and see a hint of buoyancy in their step. But as soon as I answer the door and they see my disfigured face full of scars, their entire demeanor changes. At that point, there is nothing more to do than simply begin. I want to get through the awkward phase of their stolen stares until they ingest the psilocybin, and I guide them through meeting their psyche for the first time, maybe ever. Once they come back to reality, they no longer look at my scars with disgust or fear. The compassion the mushroom brings is palpable, and once they can see themselves, they can also see me.

A glance through Amy's questionnaire reveals a refreshingly different client than my usual fare. It is primarily men who come to these retreats. Very specifically, white, middle-aged men who are brilliant at what they do and often have been atheists for most of their life. They usually followed a predictable path in their childhood: smarter than everyone in their class (and the teacher), inserting science into every Bible story, which propelled them deeper into the lab or microscope and secured their forever-future position of "the man who has the ideas and finds the answers." The thought of being the future CEO gets him through his teenage years when everyone else is at the football games or getting drunk at the party; he has his eye on the prize— the long game. In college, he generally has loosened up mainly because he finds his classes boring and unable to hold his attention, but right about then, he reminds himself that Jobs built Apple in his garage. So, who needs college, anyway? Not men. Have you ever heard of a female Silicon Valley tycoon who didn't attend college? No, you haven't. The rules of diplomacy don't apply to the male population. By the time he is entering his thirties, he is out of ideas, and a combination of ego, sex drive with no relationship skills, and an entire team of people whose lives rest on his ability to come up with the next biggest and best thing is there in place of the ever-flowing fountain of wisdom.

And so he wants to do mushrooms.

It is a desperate grab not to show his humanity, plus bonus points if later, after achieving the next most significant advancement in whatever field he is in, he can say that he had his epiphany on a psychedelic trip. His bout with experimental therapy makes him not only a genius but *relevant*. Recently, a man like this came through to have the retreat experience and "saw his soul," as he described it during the session. His walls broke down, and he was overcome with emotion as he saw all of his hurts and wounds were laid bare but covered by "a blanket of colorful love." He had a profound experience that is rare and a gift to those who encounter it: every ounce of pain that one has endured can be seen, known, and loved by a deep primal force of the universe. His core wounding needed to heal, and screaming to be seen and tended to. But when it came time to integrate this experience, it was too painful for him to look at. He became angry, dreadfully defensive, and began yelling at *me* as if I twisted the experience for him. Or blame his controlling mother or abusive father. "I didn't come here for *this*," he had shouted, pounding his fist on the table. I jumped in my seat. "Then what did you come here for?" I asked, trying to remain calm and wishing I had thought about the inevitable consequences of the rich and famous being asked to face their humanity.

"Not to be told I'm worthless by an old woman who hides in a tree house and gets off on successful men crying like babies." He left before it was all integrated.

I think about him sometimes and the countless other men who have had less aggressive but just-as-avoidant behaviors in the post-trip sessions. The ones who refuse to see the pain, to heal the wound, are out in the world, inevitably wounding others. Is this work doing more harm than good? But then there are those I know are trying, that I receive updates from, and who have joined a Buddhist sangha or felt the presence of Jesus from their flannographs from Sunday school. Maybe, just maybe, if I'm lucky, the two groups, the assholes and those that find peace, balance each other out.

This client demographic may be frustrating and scary at times, and it certainly breaks all the criteria I try to use to weed out the bad seeds. But I also know how to deal with them. I've become good at it, so I keep saying yes to their sessions. And, also, for all intents and purposes, they are my father. He was a business type in his own right, brilliant beyond belief. He was a hard worker, yet an absent father and abusive husband. He was an alcoholic, but it was socially acceptable because it was behind closed doors. My mother, caught up in her tangle of trauma and the tumultuous roller coaster of being a daughter of an alcoholic to being married to an alcoholic, did her best to shield us from him. Still, his absence was as noticeable as his presence. Both left a lonely and deep wound, turning my soul and sometimes my skin black and blue. He left my mother and me when I was in middle school on March 15th. In my poetic fantasies, I'd like to think he went on the Ides of March on purpose, a poignant and purposeful nod to killing the dictator inside of him. But alas, he left in a drunken stupor right before dinner, declaring the Beef Stroganoff to be apprehensible, and died in a car crash as he entered the exit ramp of the freeway five miles from home. My mid-life crisis male clients offer me a glimpse of the light side of my dad, who finds healing and makes amends, and the rest of the twelve steps. But sometimes, they remind me of the shadow side, too, and as dysfunctional as it sounds, they offer me some comfort as well. A point of contact to the man I never got to know.

But this Amy, she is different. On paper, she seems like an easy client: a 40-year-old woman (almost) who has been to lots of therapy (done some work on her own) and suffers from anxiety, bouts of depression, and a general feeling of unhappiness. Her biggest problem is boredom. I'll bet her kids have gone off to school all day, her husband brings in all the money, and after the first few years of cutting the sandwiches into little hearts and volunteering with the PSO, life now feels like it has come to a complete halt, and so the mushroom medicine is calling her name.

The risk of taking a client like her is that hearing her story means I must confront mine. It will be like looking into my wounded window of a life I let go of: the beautiful mundane. There will be details of the dishes, the laundry, and the car pick-ups and drop-offs. She will tell me what it's like to watch her kid play basketball, begin swim lessons, graduate, or even attend a first day of school. There might be a story about a love that had gone stale and what they did to rekindle it, or what sex was like after all these years with the same person, and if the deal-breakers ever really ended up being a big deal. This demographic, the bored housewife, posed the most significant risk to me. I could crack, exposing every shred of darkness I had yet to overcome, the longing for the life I left pouring out through my wounds. I avoided this type of client at all costs.

I shift my eyes from the computer screen to the large pine and evergreen trees growing just beyond the porch. They reach the sky, protecting Theo and me day in and day out. If I say yes to Amy, I will need to run into town, an additional trip than my comfort zone allowed because I am out of psilocybin. I am ok with once a month. Any more than that, and I get anxious. The sun is warm, but the air is crisp, and I want to see if the wind will blow even a little. The pine trees nodding in agreement will be the nudge from the universe to tell me if I should take Amy or tell her I am booked. I don't need the income this month. But as I gaze at her picture, something in her eyes makes me curious. Her happiness makes me want to test my emotional doorstep. Could I enter without losing it or running away? A little voice inside warns me not to accept her, to take Luke instead, the boutique gym designer from New Jersey, awaiting my reply. Lifting my face to the sun, I wait for the wind to blow, for a crow to caw out, or for a leaf to serendipitously fall on my face. Nothing but stillness and silence. "Ah, fuck it," I say to absolutely no one, and with a swift click of the mouse, I hit "Accept" on Amy's application.

Here goes nothing.

7
Fire

Just moments ago, I burst into existence, a product of a magnificent process: the collision of powdered glass, the transformation of red phosphorus into white, and the spontaneous ignition in the air. This volatile beginning is my gateway to survival. Nourished by oxygen, I remain aflame long enough for her to transfer me to the candle, marking the start of my journey.

The wick stood straight up, a stiff braid of cotton, all three strands tightly wound and waiting for its next life. I suppose the cotton came from a farm where leathered and worn-out hands picked it, with dirt under their fingernails and calluses from pulling the cotton bolls from the stalks. Unless a machine came along and took away the jobs, the wages, and food for the farmers and their families, all in the name of productivity. However she got here, she stood, spine-straight in a solidified, once melted, cylindrical pillar of wax.

The three strands of the wick, tightly braided, were like a prayer to the Father, Son, and Holy Ghost. They were ready to hold the dance that I, the flame, would bring. As I engulfed the end of the wick, it shrank, becoming stiffer, the tip bending forward like a hook. As it bends, I settle in, sitting at the edge of its existence where threads meet the wax. And there, I transform. No longer monochromatic, I became a vibrant blue, red, orange, and yellow canvas. I burn, I burn, I burn.

Below me, the wax begins its familiar ritual. It melts, a process it has undergone countless times before—a circular puddle forms, threatening to extinguish me. But as the tension grows, the wax pushes outward, asserting its existence. It forces wax off the edge, dripping down the wine bottle that holds me, a testament to my endurance.

The wax drips, forming a stalactite, a waxy icicle on the side of the bottle as if it will, over time, create its cave—a cave filled with stories told through drawings and language that future generations will study for centuries. All will ask what it was about: this candle and this tree house, with these words, traumas, and tears. What conclusions will they draw about humanity? I sit, dancing in the oxygen that gives me life, holding vigil for the souls coming into this room.

8
Dr. Lauren

The soft glow of the sun pouring through the window wakes me before Theo does. He must be sleepy, too. I stroke his soft head with my fingers, and he purrs in his sleep. The sheer curtains hanging from the window sway in the slight crisp breeze that floats through the opening. My entire house, set inside a large tree, is surrounded by leaves turning yellow, orange, and red as if the whole thing is ablaze.

Sundays hit differently. It is the one day a week that I am on a solo mission—totally and utterly alone with nowhere to be and no one to see. Still lying in bed, I lengthen my stiff and aching body into a full stretch, allowing a loud grunt to escape from my mouth, breaking the surrounding silence, thick like water. My grandmother's oval mirror hangs on the wall, greeting me as I sit up slowly, allowing my body to adjust upright. My hair, curly and unruly, has turned all sorts of gray, white, and silver. Sticking up and out, I attempt to tame it a bit, mostly out of habit. I won't see anyone today, so it doesn't matter. If it were my choice, I'd prefer never to see anyone again. I forced myself to see clients most days, telling myself it is good for me to interact, stay connected, and have some extra spending money. *Who knows, maybe I will escape to Europe one day.* But lately, every motivating reason I can come up with is not enough.

I bought it at the farmers market at the bottom of the hill the day I left and moved into the tree house. It was my first ritual in the new house. Upon arrival, dirt and dust covered my car from the journey up the road. I selected one box to bring into the empty house, placed it in the middle of the room, and set the candle on top. Lighting the wick, I sat cross-legged on the floor in the empty room, watching the flame dance and burn before me. The flame's brightness took over as the sun vanished behind the horizon. But I didn't care. I was in no rush. I knew this was both a beginning and an end, and as I stared at the dancing glow, I made a vow: multiple vows.   I vowed forgiveness. I vowed love. I promised to help everyone I could out of the jail their minds put themselves in. If I couldn't be free, at the very least, others should be. That first night, exhausted from moving, packing, driving, and all of the emotional weight of the days and weeks that led up to the departure, I fell asleep before I could blow the candle out. I awoke the following day to the sound of birds singing their morning songs, and there, holding vigil for me all night, the flame still burned. Out of sheer curiosity and amazement, I kept it going that day and then again that night until the candle's wax threatened to extinguish the flames watching over me. Trekking back down the hill to the market, I bought three more.

Transferring the flames from one candle to the next was ceremonial. A sacred act like that of the religious. It was only a moment, but it was also a marker. A marker of something inside me that had become extinguished and now was alight again. I didn't buy into it at first, but looking back, I realize the serendipitous flame that kept ablaze was a flicker of hope in the darkness threatening to overtake me. I left that new candle on the box, watching it burn day after day, switching it to another wax pillar when the current candle threatened the flame's existence. When my stash of candles ran out, I headed back down the hill and bought half a dozen more. Replacing the candle has become a repeated ritual, transferring *the flame* repeatedly has become my whole existence. If I let it become extinguished, then I, too, would stay lit.

I remain vigilantly aware of the threatening breeze coming in the windows, and when the flame dance becomes too intense, I lovingly cut the wick on the new candle before cradling the flame to her new home. I slowly walk, heel-to-toe, almost gliding across the floor, holding my breath when I move from room to room with *the flame* in hand. I talk to it as I do my house plants; I watch over it like my child, as I did once to my son, believing that somehow, energetically, he can feel all of this love, care, and attention I give to the flame—I cling to this hope with dear life. I have lived with this trust that sometimes feels more like grief-suffocating darkness, with only a flicker of light for 18 years. But, it has never blown out.

As the coffee warms my hands, I watch *the flame* move and dance in front of me. The wax level is getting high; I must transfer it soon. "Hi," I whisper into its ambiance. It moves slightly and then back to stillness like my son would toss and turn before fully awake. My thoughts wander to him, and what might he be doing now? Is he waking up early or sleeping on Sunday? Does he have anyone to keep him warm as the seasons change? How does he take his coffee? The pain is always right there at the surface. Sometimes, I let it in, taking over and rendering me useless for days and weeks. But I can't today. I must go down the hill to buy more candles, so once again, I slam the proverbial door on the image of my son burned into my memory. Shoving my feet into the matted fur at the bottom of my slippers, I heave myself off the velvet couch. Theo needs to be fed, anyway. The flame, ever aware of my presence, moves slightly as I walk by.

9
Jane

It's too early for the truck to be here. I glance at my wrist, my watch confirming what the dark sky whispered. With an exaggerated sigh, I put down my coffee, grab the clipboard, and go to the back of the large grocery store. This morning's delivery is butter, my favorite delivery to handle—the *best of the worst.*

"Good morning!" I greet the truck driver, who tips his hat and smiles as he yanks the back of the delivery truck upward to reveal the container's contents. The cold air from the refrigeration hits my cheeks. Growing up on the farm, my family made our butter. It was one of my mother's favorite chores. The smell of homemade bread from the kitchen foretold the afternoon snack loaded with homemade butter and a sprinkle of cinnamon and sugar.

Mondays were butter day on the farm and now, here too, at the store.. Mondays feel like home. Someone, somewhere in this Universe, must have arranged that.

Making butter is all about agitation. It separates the fat from the milk and then uses it to your advantage. Mama used to say that making butter was the best reminder that sometimes, things weren't better left alone. Sometimes, they needed to be poked, prodded, and churned into something fatty, salty, and delicious. Mama would scrunch her face up as she vigorously shook the mason jar. It was therapeutic and silly and a ritual we had together. It gave me safety and security, a type of ceremony that I carried into my adult life. If you had enough butter, Mama said, everything would be ok.

And it's here, staring at the pallets of butter, all stacked up, wrapped in cellophane, and being unloaded off a delivery truck behind an upscale grocery store in Big Bear, that I begin to cry, yet again. Instinctually, I rest my hand on my belly. There is no bump yet to speak of. I am only eight weeks along. I only found out two weeks ago, also on a Monday, but it was not a butter Monday because I was too sick to go to work that day. This Butter Monday is the first one since those two pink lines showed up on the test in the bathroom of my one-bedroom apartment. I was alone, as I imagined I would be for the foreseeable future. I had only met (and slept) with Lance once. Phone numbers were not exchanged on our night together, and to be honest, I had forgotten it had happened altogether until I was throwing up one morning in my bathroom for no good reason at all. Lance was heading through town visiting and stopped by the store as it was closing. We got to talking, and soon, we drove to the lookout spot and drank discounted wine out of the bottle in the back of his truck. I get 20% off.

It was straight out of a country song, and I loved it. I never had experiences like this when I lived at home. I didn't get invited out by boys, and by the time I could drive, the church invitations stopped and so did the forced friendship. I became aware of how lonely I really was. A night with Lance was a welcomed experience I longed for since I had overheard the popular girls talk about it in the bathroom my senior year. I swore I could hear the Dixie Chicks when I climaxed. *Cowboy take me away.* But then that was it. I got into my VW Beetle and returned to my apartment, knowing I would never see Lance again. For the first time, I felt empowered. And wanted. And now, empowerment was replaced by fear, two pink lines, and vomit that struck me any time of the day.

Lance was my third partner. My first two were in college, both long-term boyfriends that I thought possibly were "the ones." But both relationships ended on account of me. I had a glitch in my system: as soon as things got serious, and it was the logical time for the next step, the men became unattractive to me. They were utterly and inexplicably unattractive and annoying, and I could not stand to be around them for another minute. So, I always ended it. Right then and there. But here I am now. No boyfriend. No husband. No one who will stick by me. A job that gets me by, and a baby in my belly. The only person I want to tell is the only person I've ever wanted to know about anything that happened to me   my mama.

The boxes of butter become blurry as my eyes continue to fill with tears, and Jake, the dairy farm owner and now, driver, clears his throat awkwardly as he stands beside me.

"Are you…are you ok, Miss Jane?"

Jake is a gentleman through and through. He is roughly the same age as me and grew up on a farm but stayed to take over the family business. He happens to be the most handsome man I have ever seen—piercing blue eyes and small blonde curls that pile on his forehead. Even without touching them, it's clear that they are the softest ringlets known to humanity.

"Oh yeah, sorry. I was just yawning, and my eyes started to water." Half smiling, I look him in the eyes, begging him to pretend to believe me.

"If there's anything you ever need, I-"

"I know," I interrupt him. "Thank you."

I hand him the clipboard so he can sign it, and I wait impatiently to go back inside while someone else pulls these pallets into the giant refrigerator. Nodding at one another, I turn on my heel, heading back inside as fast as possible. I pick up the pace of my feet, walking briskly, head down, and go straight to the back corner of the fridge—not where the butter goes, but the eggs. Egg delivery was yesterday, so this corner offers a haven with no interruptions.

Closing my eyes, I bring forth the stored, sacred memories of her. Of them. A picture of Mama and Daisy becomes apparent—the tall grass that needed to be cut and the horses that couldn't eat it fast enough. The sun was beating down on our shoulders, and the breeze blew Mama's dark hair wildly about. She had the best laugh. Being with Mama made me feel like the most important person. Mama made everyone feel this way, but time was suspended when we were together. That life was the only life I ever wanted. Coming home to the animals, sitting on the porch with Mama, rocking back and forth in silence in the chairs Grandpa had made. Mama and I were best friends. Mama was my *only* friend. We did everything together, and then one day, Mama was gone, just like that. Tears begin to form at the corner of my eyes again when, suddenly, the light in the fridge is turned on above my head. Standing still, I wait to see if someone is coming, or perhaps the switch got turned on by mistake. Holding my breath, I hope no one will find me there. I am alone, crying in the dark of the egg cartons. The light turns off. I can facade being strong another day.

Shaking my head, I slap myself on the cheek a few times.

"Perk up, Jane. It's Butter Monday!" Like a cheerleader at a football game, I yell this loudly, walking out of the fridge and into the store's bright lights. Placing my hand on my belly again, I whisper to whoever is inside: "I got you, Poppy."

It is almost time to open, and there is all the butter you need. *Maybe, just maybe*, I think, *it will be ok.*

10
Amy

It's been a week since I sent my request to Dr. Lauren, and I'm already packing my bag. My purple suitcase with packing cubes makes it easy for my diligently rolled, Marie Kondo-inspired clothes to fit nicely. I am packing a few everyday outfits, plus a fancy, maroon-sequined jumpsuit for the day of the mushroom trip, dressing *for the job I want!* And, since I'd wear that on the Today Show, I decided to meet the mushrooms with some famous writer energy. I have clear, studded high heels to match.

Big Bear is only a four-hour drive from my house, which leaves me with a tough decision: should I listen to a depressingly sad Kristin Hannah novel on the way or drum up some medical mushroom podcasts to be ultra-prepared? It's important to me that I am the very best client Dr. Lauren has ever had.

While the whole experience will only take three days, I will be gone for a week. The plan is as follows: I'll get up to Big Bear and stay at an adorable and very Instagram-worthy Airbnb while I calm my mind and have a few days to decompress. It has a charming main street and many trails to walk and hike on. My Airbnb also has a hot tub. Then, on Wednesday, I'll head up to Dr. Lauren's house, where I'll have my psychedelic trip. Her emails say it will take 4-6 hours for the initial descent (whatever that means), then we'll have two days' worth of integrative therapy, and I will be staying in her guest room for those two days. Then, on Saturday, I will come home. *Easy peasy.*

I thought about booking another week away to write my bestselling novel. But I decided two weeks was too long to be away, and I could always write during my boring and long days when the kids are at school.

I pack a spiral notebook I got from Erin Condren for this occasion. Certainly, Dr. Lauren won't mind jotting down a few notes while I am tripping. Otherwise, how will I remember the visions, characters, and chapters that are revealed to me? Maybe this is what I will do during the "integration" phase. Dr. Lauren won't have anything to do while I write! I'm sure troubled people come to her and need tons of therapy afterward, but what about undiscovered geniuses who need space to create?

As I began to zip up my bag, I remember the two cards my kids gave me to read while I was gone. The thought of actually going away sends my heart racing. *What if a kid gets sick? Like last time?* Two years prior was the last time I left town,on a weekend trip with my girlfriends. When I called my husband on the first night, he didn't answer right away due to the stomach bug my daughter had contracted, causing her to vomit all over her bed, the hallway, and the bathroom. I had contemplated getting an Uber to take me on the two-hour trip back to my house to help her.

"Oh, that is sad," my friend said. Her face meant it, and then she did what I wished I could: she switched to reality, no other anxious thoughts entering her mind. "Well, there's nothing to do about it here. He's got it." And then, she just kept reading her book.

And he did have it. Or at least I lay awake all night in that tiny, adorable cottage and hoped he had it. I contemplated setting my timer every 15 minutes to text him and tell him to have her sip some water, but honestly, I couldn't decide if that would do more harm than good. Because, of course, she would then choke because you can't just syringe water into a sleeping mouth, and if he woke her up to sit up and sip, well, then she can't rest, which is what the body needs.

And that was how my first night away from my family went.

The next night was better. Or at least different. After another day of wine tasting and a delicious dinner out in town, the three of us returned to our quaint Airbnb, and we just stood there, shirts off, in front of the modern circle mirror in the middle of a farmhouse in West Texas. We stood together, shoulder to shoulder, contemplating our boobs. Our boobs, each other's boobs. All six of them threatened to stretch down to our belly buttons in three different sizes, shapes, and lengths. We didn't say much about them, but we all needed some witnessing of the aging woman's body.

On that trip, I was the first to wake up both mornings. The wood floors creaked as I walked, and it took me a long time to figure out where the kettle was. I was so happy there was a Chemex at the Airbnb. There was also a Keurig, but I'm way too old for that shit. It's not strong enough. I like my coffee dark and robust—one scoop of grounds per cup of water, enough to grow a few hairs on your chin. Or chest. Or both, if you are me. Sometime after childbirth, my body decided just to produce new hair, and I don't shave them except for the ones around my nipples because I am not a psychopath who dares to pluck around the nipple area.

Around the same time that the weekend trip took place, I had also started taking all these pills. My health had spun out of control ("stress-induced," is what LYZ said), and the real reason I came on the trip that weekend was to figure out what the fuck happened to my life. The rest of the weekend was exactly how I wanted it to be: relaxing and fun with friends, music, wine, and shopping. When I came home, it was everything that I wanted the reunion to be, too: my kids greeted me with hugs and squeals, my husband made dinner, and everyone loved their gifts. I felt rejuvenated for the next week ahead and able to accept, to some degree, that my life was different now than it had been ten years prior. For the next few weeks, a few new ideas came into my mind: my husband and I had sex three times a week, and I thought I might go on a run at one point, and then, all of a sudden, it stopped.

I woke up one Monday and wondered if I had made up the whole weekend. It was all gone. I was at war with reality again, was out of fresh ideas, and began the slow but steady downfall into loathing who I was and what I had become.

That was the day that I started sending out the queries. I wanted a story to tell on the Today Show about how I was at my lowest, but I kept going, like that little blue engine, and then, one day, I scored the ever-evasive book deal. *Four a day*, I told myself. *That won't be too hard, but it will be hard enough because you will feel like you are doing something.* And I did. I wrote my four "daily queries" for the next three weeks and waited.

At first, absolutely nothing happened. So, while I waited, I listened to manifesting podcasts, lit candles, and sprinkled salt around my computer, and still, I waited.

Then, the rejections started coming in—a few bites to see the whole manuscript, but nothing else. My novel doesn't know what she is or where she belongs. She is part of a million different genres (history, fantasy, fiction, speculative fiction, women's fiction, et-*fucking*-al) and can't be placed clearly on a shelf. In the end, I realized my novel is a reflection of me.

I have always been good at tiny parts of everything. I was good at painting and almost went to art school. I was half good at running but didn't push myself to improve (plus, *my thighs*). I was only okay at cooking in my early years of marriage, but then I got fat because I had no self-control, which made it hard to stick to. What I wanted to do was to be a good writer. A great writer. An *award-winning* author.

But my book didn't know what she was because I didn't know what I was, and all the rejections made that abundantly clear.

"Thank you so much for allowing us to read your manuscript, but…" I wouldn't finish the sentence after a while and instead, I'd pick up my glass of Cabernet, which didn't do what it used to. The calming effect, the euphoria, nope. Gone. Even the THC I had gotten from a pain doctor because sometimes my shoulder hurt, had lost its edge.

Completely packed, I shake the thoughts out of my head as I heave the suitcase off the bed. *Positive vibes, Amy,* I remind myself. *All of that is leading you exactly where you need to be.*

"Who's ready for some mushrooms?" my husband smiles as he enters the room, interrupting my pity party. I smile and grab my water bottle off the nightstand.

"I put dinner-"

"-in the fridge, labeled for every night you are gone. I know. You told me. And you made that video in case I have amnesia while you are gone." He's kidding. *Right? He's not going to get amnesia just out of the blue, is he?* I laugh nervously.

"Don't forget to give-"

"-vitamins, have them drink water and not overeat sugar. I got this, Amy. Try, and for once in your life, do something for yourself. Try not to worry about anything here and fully enjoy everything *there*." He's right. I can hardly escape my anxious, bored-as-fuck-with-myself mind long enough to enjoy anything, let alone believe I ever could. *This is the last time he will see this version of Amy.* I promise myself.

I take a huge gulp of my electrolyte water, suitable for hydration on a long drive, and look him straight in the eye.

"I'm going to rock the shit out of my mushroom trip," I say triumphantly.

"Atta girl!" He leans down and kisses me before picking up my suitcase and loading it into my car. I take one last look around the house. *I will come back better for you.* I want to. I need to. I have to. My life depends on it.

11
Fire

Outside the window, a dead tree trunk extends above the top of the surrounding pine forest. It is not like the others. Perched atop the chopped trunk is a red cardinal, scanning the horizon for predators. His mate and young sit, vulnerable yet protected inside their nest, the most mystifying of paradoxes. The very thing that provides safety, warmth, and shelter also exposes one's vulnerability and safety.

I don't want to, but simply by burning, I melt my own nest. I can feel the pool of wax inching up the wick. The higher it gets, the more vulnerable I become. This only happens because whoever cut the wick made it too short in the first place. It's not an exact science. The cuts are an estimate; some end up being shorter than others, and I must fight for my existence when the wick is too small. It's all a matter of timing, of chemistry, of destiny. I can only control my heat; how fast the wax responds or how long the wick is not up to me. So many hands have played a part in the fate handed to me when I arrive atop my waxy lair; they must have done everything correctly for me to survive.

This nest of white, dripping wax that I sit upon holds what is already written in the stars. Will I burn and burn, triumphant over the melting heat that threatens to drown me? Or will I fight for my existence, staying lit when it feels against the odds, only to eventually succumb to the inevitable? I am still here, yet I don't know how long I can hold on.

I am weary, and I am tired. She used to watch out for me, like the cardinal, vigilant to keep their kin alive. But now, my survival depends on hers. Will she fight for her own light, no matter the things that have led up to now? Or will she let the hot pool of wax full of memories, mistakes, regrets, and griefs inch its way up her body until she drowns in the weight of it?

If she drowns, I will too.

12
Dr. Lauren

Every green Volvo I've owned has made the same noise and felt the same inside. The wool-blended seats are always a bit itchy, yet comforting on my skin. The tweed is like the elbow patches on a famous poet's jacket. I have a set of KuKui beads hanging from the rearview mirror. I got them once on a trip to Hawaii in college. My girlfriend and I spent a week in Maui, on the beach, right by the water, eating ahi tuna. I woke up each morning and ran on the sand, watching the whales breach in the distance. I can still smell the tanning oil when I think of it. I tell my clients that, like a blueprint, our bodies store our memories. If we sit still long enough and practice being conscious enough, we can recall these memories back to the surface, and our senses ignite as if they were happening again. When I do this with my KuKui beads, the memories of that week flood my body, and I feel like I am there again. We were young. We were free. And it was at least one hundred lifetimes ago. I rub the smooth surface of the beads through my fingers and then let them go, allowing them to sway back and forth as I start the car, which gives a little lurch. I've awoken her too soon after our last excursion into town.

Coming from a long line of Volvo enthusiasts, my destiny was to own a Volvo when I turned sixteen. That one was also green. When I got married, we drove it into the ground, ultimately taking its last lurch on the side of the road. I had convinced my husband to keep it, gut it, and let me plant flowers out of the hood. But we never did replace it and decided to drive his truck around instead. Big and capable, the truck was perfect for pulling the trailer and getting hay and dirt, even if it had awful plastic leather seats that my legs stuck to during the hot summer days. I never really minded that we didn't replace the Volvo. My old one sat in our front yard, and we filled it with all sorts of fragrant and vibrant blooms: poppies and pansies, roses and sunflowers, cascading pearls and anything I could find that looked like wisteria. They were all impractical and not native, but they fulfilled something in me that I never could quite place. Seeing that repurposed Volvo day after day made me a loyalist to the brand, so when I left, I knew I needed a car and bought a used (you guessed it) green Volvo. That only lasted me five years, and it uncharacteristically died. Volvos are known for their longevity, and my first one had almost 300,000 miles on it, so albeit used, that second Volvo certainly should have had more than five years with me in her.

She was karma.

It knew I quit my life and my family and motherhood too early, so she quit early on me too. What a bitch. Not her, me. But then, given the option, I again stuck with the green Volvo; the third time was a charm. This one won't die; she is too stubborn. This one will be with me until I go first. She has to. She is the only companion I have. Besides Theo. Oh, and the fox on my mug. I know nothing about cars except what my Volvo sounds like. She quietly purrs down the dirt road, kicking up clouds behind her as we begin the road down into town for the weekly farmers market. We are on a mission, her and I. She is both my partner in crime and also my getaway car. Psilocybin is only decriminalized in California, which means I can't get into trouble for buying or using it. But I wear a wig and big glasses, mixing up the disguises because, over the past decade, the crowds of people from surrounding areas that come in for tourist things or for buying weekend homes has increased so much that I have become increasingly paranoid that I may run into someone from my past life.

Sally, my Volvo's name, knows the way to the market. I feel like I barely have to steer, that if I fell asleep at the wheel, she'd take over. Maybe, one day, just for kicks, I will lower my seat so I am in a sleeping position and then wake myself up when we get there. But for today, I will steer the wheel. Today's sky is big and beautiful, one of those days in Big Bear where you think you could get lost: the enormously tall evergreen trees, the white and impossibly fluffy clouds, and the picturesque cabins nestled behind their docks on the lake. The lake comes into full view as I circle around and down the mountain, taking my breath away. It glistens in the sun, moving with an energy all of her own, a baptism waiting. In response to her beauty, I roll down the windows and turn on and up the music, letting the air in Joni Mitchell's words out to the wind.

As I pull into the market, Joni sings out her last words of "Big Yellow Taxi" ringing through Sally's speakers: "Hey, paved paradise and put up a parking lot, La-la, la-la-la, na-na-na-na, na-na-na." *I don't want to sound old, but Joni knows. This is precisely what Big Bear has become.* Grabbing my keys, I look down at the keychain in my hand: a faded blue rabbit's foot we got on the only vacation we took as a family. The entire Grand Canyon was before us, and my boy? He wanted a rabbit's foot. And so we left with two, one for me and one for him, purple and blue. It was one of the only things I snuck out with me when I left. People who pretend to die shouldn't grab things from their room first. I rubbed the dyed foot between my finger and thumb, wishing him a life of happiness and joy and love. At best, his dad remarried, and he was young enough that he remembers none of it, but at worst, he grew up without a mother, a deep wound no one can heal.

I shut the door behind me and looked at myself more in the window's reflection: red curls. This wig looked the most ridiculous; anyone who saw it would know it was fake. I don't know if it is Joni or the glittery Big Bear Lake, but in a last-minute decision, I yank the wig off my head, throw it into the front seat, shaking out my witchy gray curls, and walking towards the market with gumption.

I spot the tent I am looking for relatively quickly: a red awning with white polka dots differing in sizes and scattered unceremoniously throughout. The sign reads: *Fire Fungi Farm.* Designed to look like a fairy-tale mushroom, it is a bit on the nose for me, but Tom, the owner, has grown on me with his unending wit and charm. Hanging from the mushroom-topped tent are linen tote bags with mushrooms and sayings like "Let that shiitake go!" and "I'm a really fun-gi." Today's table looks like the usual fare: giant, beautiful, colorful, and, in some cases, fluffy mushrooms. Tom grows them in his little garden up the hill from the market but down the hill from my house. His house is my reference point for knowing where anything is in proximity to if I want to go.

"Hi, Tom," I say before I see him.

He pops up behind a giant box of Lion's Mane mushrooms, "Hello, Lauren!" His voice is boisterous, and he is wearing the overalls he always wears, covered in dirt and patches from a previous life. I glance to see if I have spotted a new one compared to the last time I was here. I spy a Coca-Cola patch that I'm sure I haven't seen before, and I smile despite myself. I can't imagine this hippie, "fun-gi," drinking high fructose corn syrup made by the Corporate Machine. His cheeks are rosy, and his beard is long and white: a bohemian Santa Claus if I ever saw one.

I can't help but smile back at him. "I know, I know. Are you surprised to see me so soon?"

"Don't tell me you have gotten in the habit of taking the mushrooms for yourself." He grins with a smirk…and a wink.

"I solemnly swear that I still have yet to try it." I smile, holding up three fingers in a scout's honor.

"Why is that?" he asks, his smile fading slightly. I honestly don't know why he is taking this personally.

"I-I don't know, Tom," I begin, instantly regretting saying yes to Amy and thus needing to come down here on a Tuesday when Tom decides we should exchange feelings.

"Say no more," he says, holding up his hand in a stop motion. "I get it. I have a past I want to forget, too." He picks up another box of mushrooms, Turkey Tail, as his scribbled handwriting on the front of the box declares. Placing it down, he rests his muscular and worn-out forearms on the edge of the box, looking me straight in the eye. They are soft, his voice lowered and genuine, "I broke my number one rule, Lauren. I got into my customer's business, and I shouldn't have. I hope you'll forgive me."

"Oh, Tom! It's going to take a lot more than that to scare me away," I say jokingly, trying to ease the tension my body has latched on to.

He smiles, letting the whole thing go. "What can I get for you today, then Lauren?"

"Well, it looks like you aren't the only one breaking rules, Tom," I say, wringing out my wrists. I offer some personal anecdotes on his behalf, which are also strange to me. Even though his prying questions agitated me, they riled up my nervous system, and I enjoyed it. I can't remember the last time someone asked anything about me, even if it was only three words.

"I said "yes" to an extra client. She arrives in three days and is not my typical type."

Much like the lake, Tom's eyes glitter with mischief and delight. "Ah, I see. So you not only need more, you want something different?"

"Yes. The giant mushroom that my usual, career-driven city boy likes to just take a bite out of doesn't seem like it will be this woman's flavor if you know what I mean. She's the Instagram type, so something more visually appealing, maybe?" I hear the words come out of my mouth, and I can't believe it. *Am I really changing my tried-and-true methods for some woman I have never met?* I know I am not the most stable human being on the planet, but I at least know *myself*, right?

Tom raises a finger and quickly slips behind the tent siding, leaving me to stand in a sea of mushrooms, hoping no one will come and ask me questions about what each one does.

I wait about five minutes when it starts to rain, and people duck under tents to stay dry. About ten or so people cram under the red polka dot roof, and we stand, shoulder to shoulder with one another and the mushrooms. Standing right next to me is a small family with a toddler in the stroller, an older woman who has purchased hand-dyed yarn from Janice, who lives in town, and a small, happy dog with her. As someone is about to make small talk, Tom returns from the downpour, drenched from head to toe.

"Oh, hello, weary customers. Can I offer anyone a sample?" Everyone laughs because they think he is joking, but Tom is not. He would easily eat a mushroom right out of that box.

"Excuse me," I say, trying to slink past the old woman and her happy dog so I can finish my transaction with Tom and leave. There are too many people in way too close proximity for me.

"Lauren, I'm so sorry. I don't have what I thought I did, nor do I have any. If you catch my drift, you are my only Magic customer, so I only bring them on the last Sunday of the month."

Damn. My face falls, and it is the first time in a long time that I feel nervous and unprepared for a client. I picture Amy's picture, that laugh that must be contagious, and something inside of me wants this experience to be great for her.

"Could I come to your house and get them?" I can't believe I asked him that, and from the looks of it, he can't either. For the first time, this mushroom Chris Cringle stammers on his words, "Uh-um-um sure. I don't think this rain will last too long. So how about you meet me at my house in about an hour?" He slips me his business card with his address printed at the bottom as *if I didn't already know where he lived.* Taking it, I shove it into my pocket, nod in agreement, and run out into the rainstorm.

***

Tom's house is nothing I thought it would be. Tucked at the end of a long driveway covered by trees, his home boasts nothing but charm. This little cottage is feminine and adorable for a man who lives alone: painted a delicate yellow with white trim and a red door, and a white picket fence with flowers lining the outside perimeter.

Giving myself one last look in the mirror, I get out of Sally and approach the front door. He opens it before I can knock.

"Lauren! Come on in." He is out of breath.

Hesitantly but also overcome with curiosity, I step inside a bright, open-concept living area. It's bohemian, shabby chic. I gasp when I see the white canvas couch with a million pillows that seem like you could sink right in and never get up again. Everything in the house is the opposite aesthetic Tom presents himself as.

"I know. It's not what you pictured, is it?" He chuckles behind me, shutting the door quietly.

"My, uh, sister decorated it for me. She's one of those big fancy designers out in Los Angeles, and she showed up one weekend with her entire crew and said I'd be doing her a favor if I let her decorate it for me."

"It's gorgeous!" I gush. The walls, divided into two sections, make the room feel roomier than it is. The bottom half has wainscoting, and the top half has baby blue and white stripes going up the walls and onto the ceiling. A large chandelier hangs in the middle of the room.

"Where did you get that?" I ask, pointing to the big wooden box hanging from the ceiling with large gold chains. From the center of the box are mason jars of multiple shapes, sizes, and lengths, the innermost core lit up by lightbulbs on the inside.

"Oh," Tom says with a grin. "I made that."

I turn to stare at him, my mouth hanging open despite my futile attempts to keep it shut. "And here I thought you only knew about mushrooms," I say, diverting my eyes as soon as they lock with his.

"About that. I am sorry I didn't have what you needed today, but I'm glad you're here," Tom mumbles as he walks out of the room, and I suppose I should follow.

He meanders past his kitchen (navy blue cabinets and gold fixtures) and dining room (with a gorgeous, circular table that I assume he also made) and into a hallway with a door at the edge. As he walks, he flips a switch that turns on the wall sconces, which look like outside street lamps with a retro lightbulb inside each one.

Remind me to get his sister's number.

Tom opens the door and steps down twice into a musty, somewhat predictable garage, more aligned with what I expected Tom's aesthetic to be. It is dark, except for one bulb hanging from a giant string, which turns on once you pull on it. And that he does. The small light-flow reveals two tennis balls hanging from the ceiling to let drivers know when to stop their car as they enter. Tom's truck is out front.

"Oh, sorry. I'm not used to having anyone else here. It must feel dark and stuffy." *Is he nervous?* He presses the garage door button, and the door slowly opens, creaking the whole way up.

"Ah ha!" Tom shouts and holds up a gardening tool I have never seen before. "Follow me," he says as he opens a door that leads into the famous mushroom garden I've heard stories about.

The minute I step through the door, I am Alice in Wonderland. Vines crawl up the side of the house, and the mushroom garden is more extensive than I ever imagined. "How many acres is this?" I ask, my mouth hanging open for the second, or was it the third, time?

"The lot I own is three acres. But my mushrooms only take up half an acre." He smiles, waving his hand flippantly into the vast green in front of him. I admit my tree house brings spooky vibes, but it is also unique and could be charming had I had a decorator sister who needed a favor. But this? This is amazing.

Tom has land for what seemed like days and the views! The views are so beautiful they almost seem fake. As far as the eye could see, pine trees cover the mountains like a blanket, tucking in every twist and drop and uphill, like I used to tuck my son into bed at night. *Snug as a bug in a rug!* All the trees came to a point to meet the base of the mountains shaded in various purples and blues.

"You should see them in late summer. The sunset never ends." Tom is beside me; I feel his arm brushing mine; if I wanted, I could extend my fingers to touch his. But I don't. Want to, that is.

I close my eyes and imagine what that must be like— purples, pinks, oranges, and yellows, all in a watercolor masterpiece. Then I open them again.

"She's leaving us, you know," I say, pointing at the *almost* full moon that is rising in the sky.

"Who is?" Tom asks, hand covering his eyes to search the horizon for someone I see, but he doesn't.

"The moon. 8cm every year. Pretty soon, she will be out of our orbit, and all we will be left with is the sun."

"Says *who*?!" Tom bellows with bewilderment.

"The scientists, that's *who!*" I smile back, playfully pushing his shoulder.

"Never put too much stock in science, Lauren. You gotta *feel* it to know it."

"Spoken like a true peddler of psychedelics," I say, folding my arms across my chest. I could stay here, looking at this view, talking to him all night.

"Ah, come on now. Psychedelics are science." He begins to meander again, this time through the rows of mushrooms. I follow, careful not to step on any of the budding spores.

"The science is in the soil. Whatever soil it's grown in

creates the magic it holds." He bends down to a plot of smaller mushrooms, which I recognize as the ones I've given my former clients. I bend down, too.

"This soil, it's the best stuff there is. It's been regeneratively grown and packed with nutrients. It's the only soil that I will grow my psilocybin in."

"How did you get it here?" I'm asking if he is telling me the truth or has decided to pull one over on me.

"It took me three years to tend to the land," he says, a sorrow hanging in the corners of his words that I can't quite place.

"Of course it did. That makes perfect sense: that you, the mushroom man, who lives in a Southern Living magazine set against the backdrop of every calendar of Big Bear, took three years to make the perfect soil for an illegal drug." There goes my mouth, hanging open again.

"Ah, it's not illegal now. At least not here. You are lucky; I would have loved to use the mushrooms in my therapy practice back in the day." He stands up abruptly, mushrooms in hand, and begins walking back toward the garage.

"I didn't know you were a therapist," I say, shocked and embarrassed that I knew almost nothing about this person I might consider a friend. Until today, I had only driven past his house, didn't know he had a sister, and was utterly unaware of his past life before he grew mushrooms.

"Yeah, I don't talk about it much. I made some mistakes on the job when I was young and prefer to keep them in the past." We lock eyes, and for the first time in a long time, I feel a deep connection of empathy and understanding with someone other than my clients.

"As you said back at the market, *I have a past I want to forget, too*," I say. He sticks out his hand, and we shake on it. Our hands remain clasped together in mid-air for awkwardly longer than they should, only to be interrupted by my phone alarm ringing.

Oh shit. The candle.

"You got somewhere to be?" Tom asks, heading back into the garage. "Uh, no," I stammer. "I just need to get back and feed my cat, Theo." I am wringing my wrists again—a nervous habit. I have never been away from the candle for this long; it is a practice that I hold very sacred. Of course, the alarm is for fire safety, but somewhere deep down inside of me, I also believe the only reason I am still alive is because the flame keeps on burning. What would I do, and who would I be if it blew out?

"I was going to offer you a cup of tea or pint of beer while I put these in the dehydrator…" he trails off, placing the mushrooms inside a giant white box with knobs and buttons and lights.

"Tom," I say, more agitated than I want to, "this seems like the same psilocybin you've always given me. Is this going to be worth it or what?" My cheeks are hot, and I feel embarrassed from lashing out at him like this. His face falls.

"It's ok, go on. I can bring them to you when I'm done. You're in that tree house at the top of the hill, right?"

"Yeah!" I scream, my head already out the window of my car, and I am peeling away, dirt clouding up behind me, covering Tom, standing in his driveway, hurt and confused.

That makes two of us.

13
Jane

My day off was glorious, and I wish I had four more. The exhaustion that has made a home deep inside of me is incomprehensible. Overnight, acne and dark circles replaced my youthful glow, and my pants were increasingly more challenging to pull on. Today, I resort to a hair tie to hold the waistband closed. The only plus side to this whole body makeover is that, for the first time in my life, I have boobs.

And I love it.

I've always been flat-chested and grew to accept it as soon as padded bras came to my attention when I was in college. My roommate introduced them to me, and they were the best thing I had ever seen since sliced bread. But now, I need to buy new bras because these push-ups make my boobs feel like they will hit my chin or spill out the side. *Put that on your shopping list.* I make a mental note as I adjust the straps to my sports bra and head into work.

Today is, unfortunately, not butter day. Today, I am in produce, helping the local farmers bring fresh crops that didn't sell at the Farmers Market the day before. Since we take a cut of their sales, we prefer to give them a chance at the market before selling it on our shelves. I check my list, and we have all the usual vendors: Sally, who will bring in carrots, broccoli, cauliflower, and snap peas; Jeremy, who specializes in asparagus, beets, and corn; and then, my personal favorite, Jen who owns a peach, strawberry, and cherry farm. Sometimes, at the end of the season, Jen will bring me a homemade pie of each of her fruits, and I invite her over for a slice (or three) a la mode.

Under these names, there is another that I have never seen on the list before, Tom, who sells mushrooms.

"Hey John," I wave my fellow manager over beside me. In the middle of stacking watermelons, he makes sure they are steady and then walks over to me.

"What's up?" he asks, looking over my shoulder at the list on the clipboard in my hands.

"Did you know this guy was trying to sell mushrooms here?" I ask, pointing to his name on the checklist.

"Oh yeah, Tom. He's a good friend of Jake's, and last week, Jake asked if I could do him a favor and get Tom in the line-up."

"I wasn't aware there was a big market for these kinds of mushrooms," I say, glancing at the list. The list doesn't have the usual cremini or button, but exotic names like Beech, Enoki, King Oyster, and Lion's Mane.

"Look, me neither. I only like mushrooms on my pizza. But the guy is paying for the spot, and any friend of Jake's is a friend of mine." He shrugs and heads back to the watermelon tower he is expertly building. He probably grew up playing Legos.

Alright then. As I clear a place for Tom and his mushrooms, I feel a tap on my left shoulder. Startled, I jump and turn around quicker than I intended to. A small woman, about 5 inches shorter than me and at least ten years older, stands before me, giving me a slight wave with her hand.

"Sorry to scare you," she says, laughing nervously and adjusting her bangs with manicured fingers. "Can you please tell me where I can find some items on my list? I am from out of town."

I scan the list quickly, hoping to rattle off a few aisle numbers that she will remember. It is store protocol to "escort" someone to their destination, but my feet are killing me, my back hurts, and a headache behind my eyes is brewing. Plus, I am starving. Her list is pretty basic: some fruits, vegetables, snack foods, and toiletries. As I am calculating where to send her first and hoping she has a pencil, so she can write down all the aisle numbers, a large sound clamors next to me, causing me to jump in surprise for the second time today. "Woah!"

"Sorry about that, Miss," a middle-aged gentleman wearing overalls with a long white beard tips his hat at me. "I am looking for where you want me to put my mushrooms."

The noise, I now see, was caused by pounds upon pounds of mushrooms dropped to the ground in plastic crates.

"Hi, you must be Tom," I say, consulting my list. I turn to the woman, "Can you please wait one second? I am sorry." She nods eagerly, actually stepping *closer* to me like a lost puppy. I scoot closer to Tom and stick out my hand to introduce myself.

"I'm Jane, one of the managers here. It's nice to meet you." He eagerly shakes my hand, and I can feel the dirt loosen from his palms and onto mine. As soon as we pull apart, I wipe my hand on the side of my pants.

"Sorry," he chuckles, noticing my not-so-discreet attempt to wipe my hand clean.

"You know, legend has it that if you keep the mushroom dust on your hands and smell it while making a wish, it will surely come true." He points to my hand that is mid-wipe, "Go on, there's still some left I'm sure. Take a whiff." He is raising his eyebrows up and down, and because this day can't get any weirder, I take my hand off my jeans, bring it to my nose, and inhale deeply. The second the smell hits my senses, my stomach churns, and the urge to vomit all over Tom and his mushrooms takes over. I spin around as fast as I can, push the woman who has moved even closer to me out of my way, and book it to the bathroom.

***

I have never been much of a germaphobe; it is one of the many things a farm will do to you. I've delivered baby goats, mucked the stalls of horses, and drank milk straight from the bucket. But this? My face hovering over a toilet bowl in a public bathroom where more than 3 million visitors frequent every year has put me on an entirely different level of germ awareness.

I hear the door open and the sound of high heels walking toward the closed door where I sit on the bathroom floor. "Jane?" a voice I do not recognize calls out to me. My first instinct is to hide. But where? I break into a cold sweat, but she has already seen me seated on the grimy tile. But still, I don't answer. I sit like the rabbits who stop in their tracks and believe no one can see them. If I can't see this mystery woman, maybe she can't actually see me.

She knocks on the stall door and slides a pack of Ginger chews underneath, landing at my hips. "I swore by those when I was pregnant with all three of my babies." She doesn't move, her high heels planted firmly in the tile as if she got stuck in cement just as it hardened.

"Thanks," I mutter, grabbing a piece of toilet paper from the dispenser, wiping my forehead, and then my mouth. I open the bag and begin to suck on one. Adjusting myself, I lean back against the wall and, before settling in, manage to unlock the stall door and allow it to swing open slightly, revealing the woman with the pretty nails that I can't seem to get rid of.

"It helps almost instantly, doesn't it?" She hands me a bag of frozen peas that I eagerly put on my forehead.

"Does it get any better?" I ask, eyes closed; the lights are too bright. To my surprise, she sits down next to me in ripped, studded jeans, high heels and all, like we've been best friends for life. Like there we were, in the middle school bathroom, mending one another's broken hearts.

"Well, it depends. They say it should stop around 14 weeks, but one of my children lasted the entire pregnancy. How many weeks are you?" I can feel the ginger chew and frozen peas doing their job: the nausea has worn off, my body temperature is returning to normal, and my senses are, too. *How does she know that I am pregnant? Will she tell anyone?* I fight the urge to hurry away from her yet again and begin to think of a story about bad meat I ate the night before. But the panic has got me sweating again and instead, all I can barely get out is, "How did you know?"

"Oh, girl!" She puts her hand on my arm, her diamond bracelet swinging back and forth. "Are you kidding me? No one turns that green from smelling mushrooms unless they've recently peed on a stick and saw two pink lines."

I peek up at her, and she smiles at me. A calm covers me like a warm blanket after getting caught in the rain. My shoulders loosen down my back, and relief floods through to the tips of my toes. This must be what it feels like to be known and seen by someone who has been in the exact place you are standing right now. This, I realize, is the presence of a mother.

"I'm Amy," she says, skipping formality. Instead of holding out her hand to shake it, she wipes my now-dampened bangs from my forehead and blows a soft breath on the last beads of sweat that have settled at the top of my forehead.

"I'm Jane," I say, accepting her kindness in a way that surprises me. I didn't know how good this type of love would feel.

"I assume you haven't told anyone?" She says, shifting her weight by pulling her knees into her chest and resting her elbows on them. I shake my head no.

"Don't worry; I've got you covered." I look up at her, my eyes no longer hurting from the overhead lights, and she winks at me.

"What did you tell them?" I am shocked beyond belief that this woman I just met covered for me in front of my coworkers. I may not have grown up in a religious household, but a lie was one thing my dad never put up with, which is why I've ignored his calls for the past week.

"I told them I saw you last night at Whiskey Dave's doing a ski shot and having too much fun." I laugh at her attempt; Whiskey Dave's is the most Instagrammable bar in town—the last place I would ever go. On the outside it's a hole in the wall, but ever since Dywane "The Rock" Johnson walked in a few years ago, the place has blown up and is filled with tourists every night of the week. It's probably the only bathroom worse to puke in than this one.

"Well, they will either not believe you one bit or think I have a double life." I felt less like the world was ending and more like I needed a snack.

"Yeah, but even if they don't, they're men. The last thing they will think is that you're pregnant." She places her hand on my knee and squeezes it.

"Thank you," I say as tears form in my eyes and roll down my cheeks. I am not entirely sure why I am crying; hormones, of course. But also a mix of embarrassment for leaving Tom high and dry and throwing up in front of a stranger coupled with the deep grief that has always been there but only now is being vocal.

"Oh, don't worry, your pretty little head. This will pass, I promise. I already bought the chews, so you keep them with you." She stands up and offers her hand to help me off the floor. I grab one hand and use the other to hold the toilet seat, and between these two supports, I am standing up again.

"You said you were visiting. Where are you staying?" I scrub the invisible germs off my hands and spend an extra minute with bubbles and hot water to remove the smell of the mushrooms.

"My husband booked me an Airbnb on the lake. It's gorgeous, has these wall-to-ceiling windows, and is steps from the water," she says, also scrubbing away the bathroom floor, paying extra attention to the space under her diamond ring.

"Oh, I think I know the one," I say quietly as my cheeks turn into the shade of turnips. If she only knew what my small, one-bedroom, older-than-old apartment looked like. The house she is staying in is famous in Big Bear as being the most luxurious property available for rent. The views were unparalleled; the shower was like stepping into a hidden cave, and the three bedrooms boasted white linen and bear skin rugs. At least, this is what the Airbnb pictures showed. I knew three nights in this house was more than my month's rent. And probably grocery budget.

I hand her a paper towel, and as she flicks her wrist, water droplets accidentally hit the mirror. "Thank you. I'm here alone in this huge, lonely, and quiet house. Would you like to come over for dinner? I hear the sunsets are rather amazing this time of year."

She is standing too close to me again, but this time, it comforts me and feels like an invitation, not an annoyance. I feel strangely connected to her. If I go home after my shift, a package of Top Ramen, a few old bell peppers, and a half-eaten tub of hummus will greet me. I will watch a ridiculous TV show until I fall asleep on the couch and wake up disoriented and thirsty in the middle of the night, feeling alone and afraid.

"Yes, I would love that. Can I bring anything?" I gave her a small smile, thankful for the invite and grateful that someone else now knows my secret.

14
Amy

I unnecessarily and ceremoniously step on each round tree trunk leading up to the door. The door is pure glass, the only thing you'd have when your house is beautiful enough that you want others to look inside. I shudder at the contrast of my own home: messy, unkempt, out of date. I put down the bags of groceries I am holding and stop to take a selfie in front of the house. It's a black and wood modern A-frame with chic skylights, not from the 80s, and a panel of rocks meets the slanted roof. The lighting is perfect, and I frame myself from the top to avoid a double chin situation. I immediately post it with the hashtags #selfcare #retreat #alonetime.

Stepping into the house is nothing short of breathtaking. I make a mental note that before I leave, I need to do a video tour or maybe even an Instagram reel of the magical moments that people love to see: coffee by the glittering water, steam coming from the mosaic shower, my feet peeking into the corner of the frame as I lie on the bed and look out at the panoramic views. But now, I need to get ready for my guest.

Unpacking the groceries, I think about Jane and her baby. I remember the early days of being pregnant, especially with the first one, and how jarring it was that something so small could take over your entire body. I purchased salmon, white rice, brussel sprouts, all pregnancy-safe foods that help with brain development. I also got bread, which I will skip because of my thighs, and then I plan to make a hot fudge Sundae for dessert. Even though she isn't drinking, I got myself a bottle of my favorite Cab and promised I'd only drink one bottle before my trip. I want to be in a clear-headed space.

I prepare the dinner by letting the salmon sit at room temperature while the oven heats up, washing the brussels, and soaking the rice. I am going with a simple lemon and dill seasoning for the salmon and an orange and maple syrup with butter sauce on the brussel sprouts. I soaked the rice because everyone knows that it carries high levels of lead, and soaking gets rid of it—or at least that is what that influencer "doctor" said.

I want everything to be full of flavor and perfect for Jane. I don't know her story, but she wasn't wearing a ring and could come to a stranger's house at the last minute. So, I think no one is cooking for her on the regular. The table at the Airbnb is a handmade, wooden piece that sits in the middle of the massive, planked porch. I decided that sitting at the end of the table closest to the house but facing the water was the best choice. When it is time for dessert, we can always move to the Adirondack chairs on the dock and stargaze while we eat the ice cream. My phone buzzes in my pocket, and I get a text from my husband: "Everything is great here! Just making sure you checked in with no problems!"

I double-tapped to put a heart on the text and snapped a quick picture of the view to send back.

"I did, and it's stunning! Thank you again so much for holding down the fort!" I add a mountain emoji.

"I love you! Have fun, and don't worry about a thing!"

I smile and put the phone into my pocket. I decide not to tell him I am having Jane over for dinner. There would be lots of talk about *how do I know she is not a psychopath killer?* Or worse, *Of course, you found someone to mother while on a solo trip.* And I guess he would have a point. It is not like my anxious brain to take a chance on someone I don't know. But seeing her on the floor of that disgusting bathroom in a cold sweat made me feel so sorry for her. Plus, once a mother, always a mother.

I find a floral tablecloth in the linen closet and use the matching napkins. The plates and silverware are fancier than my holiday set at home, so the table doesn't need much to make it look special. I arrange two bouquets I purchased at the store, one for the centerpiece and the other for the kitchen. I put two candles on either side of the flowers but wait to light them until I can be around them the whole time. I'd hate for this place to catch on fire.

As I tend to the food in the kitchen, I become aware that I am doing the same thing I do at home, just in a different location. The knife moves through the onion and the brussel sprouts, like it's on the self-drive setting of my Tesla at home. I've done this a thousand times. There has been much in my life that I am thankful for; that went the way I wanted it to: maybe even better than I thought it could. I love being a mom; my kids are *the joy* of my life. I love my husband and the life we have built together. I find a deep sense of satisfaction in these things, even happiness. But these are all roles that I play. When I think about who I am, my writing talents, or the ways I have believed in myself repeatedly, but still kept coming up short, I feel sick.

My knife stops mid-cut. And right there, in the lap of luxury, over a wooden cutting board that probably cost more than my outfit, I begin to cry. Small tears at first, running down my cheeks and minorly clouding my vision, but then, a dam snaps inside of me, and a deep, throaty scream finds its way out of my mouth, and I begin to sob. Kneeling, I sit with my knees pulled into my chest, and I let myself go. No one is here to try and fix it; my children don't have to feel like they need to comfort me. No one can even hear me. Finally, it's me and only me.

"*FUUUUUUUUUUCK!*" I scream as loud as I can, banging my fists on the ground. "Fuck, fuck, fuck!" I can't help it, but I begin to think of everything that has gone wrong over the past ten, no, fifteen years of my life, and they start piling up like stacks of Taylor Swift albums, with all my eras laid bare. Like a bad montage from a movie, I see myself in the scenes that, yes, I made it through, but I am angry I had to. They are heavy and weigh me down, pushing me to the ground until I am lying, face up, in the middle of the kitchen floor of this ridiculously lavish house.

What a waste. I think. "What a fucking waste," I say aloud to no one. To myself. Who deserves that gorgeous shower and a lakeside patio? Plenty of women have earned this in a million different ways that I have not. I make no income; I have no accomplishments to celebrate. The things I do at home and for the people in it are merely survival tasks. Nothing I do or have ever done is extraordinary. I cover my face with my hands and try to breathe in deeply and slowly, reminding myself how traumatic it would be for the kids if I were found dead in this home. And then it hits me: *I am a damn fool.*

I couldn't kill myself even if I tried. It wouldn't work out. I would make a mistake, and then I'd be in the hospital having to answer a million questions about why I tried to do what I did and having to face the reality that I failed. At yet another thing. A new bath of tears and screams come wailing out of me. I feel so stupid. I keep trying against all odds. I do everything I've been told to do, yet here I am, empty-handed. I desperately wanted to show my kids they could make a decent living doing what they love. I wanted them to believe in the things they love and that they could build a life around them that brings them joy. By getting good at their craft, they could stick a middle finger to the man and be the one with the exact life they had ever dreamed of.

I failed. I failed myself, little Amy, who had dreamed of being a published author since she was ten, and worse, I failed my kids. My worst nightmare is coming true right before my eyes: my kids will look back one day, and when someone asks what their mom did for a living, they will say, "She tried to be an author, but I guess she couldn't do it." And I will have to live with that reality, too.

My hands tremble as I wipe away the tears and snot accumulating on my now puffy face. I feel sick to my stomach, the nausea rising in my throat. I roll to my side, open the freezer drawer at the bottom of the fridge unit, and pull out an ice cube. Sticking your head in a bowl of freezing ice water resets your vagus nerve or something. I don't know what a vagus nerve is, and I don't have the sea legs to get up and prepare a whole bowl, but I grab a single ice cube and begin rubbing it all over my face, allowing the cold water to bring some relief. As the ice does its job, my tears slow their rolls, and I can feel myself breathing again. I am not used to this level of vulnerability, even with myself. Even when I met with Lyz, I kept things civilized and made myself very "put together." The shame of who I've turned out to be runs so deep that to open Pandora's box, even the tiniest crack, feels like it can ruin me. And judging by this brussel sprouts breakdown moment, I am correct.

The ice cube is melted, and I stick the tiny sliver on my forehead, where my third eye chakra would be, knowing this will do nothing to solve my problems. I shut the freezer door with a slam and get to my feet, wobbly but able to stand and take a deep breath. Walking to the circular mirror on the wall, I see myself: raccoon eyes and the-night-after-hair, with fifteen pounds more than I want to be there. With a sigh, I turn my head to look at the clock; *oh shit*. Jane will be here any minute. But before I can jolt to the bathroom to put back on my polished persona, the doorbell rings.

Damn that glass monstrosity! She is staring right at me with a hesitant smile and a small wave that is only reserved for when you catch an (almost) middle-aged woman having a midlife crisis. I lick the sides of my middle finger and begin to wipe the mascara furiously from under my eyes, and even though she can see me clear as day, I fall to my hands and knees and crawl into the hallway to the bathroom. "One minute!" I cry in a sing-song voice.

If she had any mind about her, she would leave. Immediately.

After I collect myself, smoothing my hair up into a messy bun, splashing cold water on my face, and pinching my cheeks for a bit of natural rouge. Taking a deep breath, I stand straight up and give a big, performative smile in the mirror. *It's time to be who she needs you to be.* I keep the smile plastered on, the tears buttoned up, and I reach the front door. She's still standing there, looking vulnerable and hesitant, holding a bouquet of bright flowers.

"Hi, Jane!" I say, over-enthusiastically, swinging the door wide open.

"Hi," she pauses. I feel bad for her; she obviously can't decide whether to bring up the breakdown she just witnessed or pretend it didn't happen. I begin to ramble in an effort to make the choice for her. I certainly will be pretending nothing happened.

"These are beautiful! I love fresh flowers, don't you? Come on in! I have started dinner; I hope you like salmon. They say that omega-3's are great for the baby's brain." I am talking so fast I see spit flying from my mouth in the sunlight.

What a great impression.

A bead of sweat rolls down my back; I am anxious. I don't let people see the parts of me I am embarrassed about. Vulnerability, I have learned, is a door to being manipulated. You show your weakness, and that the exact place they will target. This has happened too often; I learned the hard way and it's better to keep my cards close to my chest with my heart not anywhere near my sleeve. Jane has already seen more of me than any friends back home, and I feel dreadfully exposed. I can feel my heart rate increasing, and I am pitting out in my new Anthropologie shirt. I feel as though I can't breathe. *Take a deep breath. Inhale, exhale.* I repeat this to myself as I arrange the flowers in a vase I found in the cupboard. *Don't cry. Don't cry.*

"This is such a beautiful house. Have you stayed in it before?" Her sweet voice interrupts my panic, forcing me to switch gears.

"This is my first time in Big Bear! I live in Newport Beach, but we never make it up here. Did you grow up around here?"

Ok, we are moving towards normal. I feel a rising satisfaction as I place the vase of flowers on the table.

"No, I grew up in Redlands. Have you been?" She rests her hands on the counter and swallows.

"Oh, I'm sorry, you want some water? I have sparkling, or still, or fruit-infused." She stares blankly at me.

"Regular?" she says with a small laugh, tucking hair behind her ear.

"I went to Redlands once to visit for college. My dad really loved the idea of the University of Redlands, but it wasn't really my vibe. There was too much farming and not enough beach." I laugh and hand her a regular ol' water bottle. She drinks half of it immediately.

"Excuse me," she says. "Does being pregnant make you thirsty?" There it is. I see it for the first time: her incredible youth and the fear and trepidation of wading these waters.

"Jane, I don't mean to pry, but who else knows about the baby?" I close the oven and set the timer. She looks down at her hands, her cheeks blushing and shoulders slouching. Suddenly, she seems so small, so tender, so *vulnerable*. Immediately, my mama bear instinct kicks in. I know what to do now. I know how to take care of her, how to mother her, and how to help her. I can do this role all day long. It's the friendship piece that I can't step into. This realization relaxes my entire body. I feel my shoulders release the tension they held, and I put my hand lightly on her shoulder. She begins to cry.

"No one," she says almost in a whisper. "Not even the man I slept with that got me here."

"Have you seen a doctor yet?" My hand moves in light circles around the top of her shoulder, the same movement I did when my babies were babies, and I would attempt to get them back to sleep or soothe the pain of a wounded knee.

"No. I-I can't decide if I want to keep her." She says it like an apology.

"Come on, let's go on the porch and get some fresh air." She follows me outside to the wood-planked porch, surrounded by panoramic views of the lake, the mountains, and infinite numbers of trees and clouds. The air is thin and breathable, a stark contrast to the Orange County smog. I gesture towards a chair at the table that I had perfectly set.

"I don't have a doctor here. I haven't lived here very long and haven't had the time to set one up." I see her relax a bit into the chair.

"Redlands isn't that far. Why don't you just go to your doctor back home?" I breathe in deeply, inhaling the clean air and exhaling the satisfaction I feel for helping her solve this problem.

"I can't go home without visiting my dad. That wouldn't be right."

"Ah, and you're not ready to tell your dad. Is he the religious type?" I say it as if I am not, which I most certainly am. But again, I'm here as a non-biased mother figure. Before she can answer, I add, "What about your mom?" I hold my breath like a stepmother who is hoping she, too, is called "mom" on Mother's Day.

"She died when I was young." She chokes on her words.

"Oh, honey. I am so sorry. Come here." Standing up, I wrap my arms around her, holding her close. She begins to cry into my shoulder, and my hand immediately returns to the circular motion on her back. After a few moments, we pull apart, and I help wipe the tears away from her eyes.

"I'm only here a few days," I say, holding her shoulders and catching her gaze, "but I want to help you in any way I can." I squeeze her shoulders and smile a warm and comforting smile, which she returns before breaking our embrace and sitting back in the sun-filled chair.

Quickly changing the subject, she asks, "Why are you in town? It's not quite tourist season." And she's right. Summer and winter see the heaviest traffic. With fantastic skiing and water skiing, Big Bear was an easy weekend escape for city-goers like me.

"Promise you won't judge?" I plead.

"Really?" she says with shock, her mouth hanging open, her hand pointing at her belly.

She has a point. In the short amount of time we have known one another, I have seen her vomit, she's seen me cry, and vice versa.

"Okay," I say, "I'm going on a three-day psychedelic trip experience."

I pause, waiting for her reaction. Nothing.

"You know, like taking mushrooms to have an otherworldly encounter. There's a lady that lives here, somewhere in the mountains." I wave my hand indiscriminately to the vast landscape next to me. "And she's a psychotherapist who guides your journey. Then, after, you have three days of therapeutic integration to try and make sense of what you experienced." Saying it aloud made it seem much crazier than it had when I signed up.

"Groovy," she says with a smile, holding up her two fingers like a peace sign. I can't help but crack a smile.

"Have you ever done mushrooms?" I ask, almost certain that I already know the answer.

"Nah. I'm from Redlands, remember?" She smiles and takes another sip of her water.

"Once a farm girl, always a farm girl?" I wink at her. "I grew up in Newport Beach and have never stepped foot on a farm. Do you miss it?"

"I miss my dad. I miss our cows, and sometimes, I used to go for a whole day without seeing another human." Jane lets her head hang back, the sun hitting her face, her eyes closed but squinting nonetheless.

"Well, then, how did you end up here?" I wondered, realizing I had yet to pour myself a glass of wine.

"After college, I wanted to try and do it on my own. My dad said he didn't need my help, which I am still unsure I believe. I foolishly thought Big Bear would be quiet and restful, but it isn't the respite I hoped it would be."

"But you found love?" I inquire, tip-toeing back into the topic of her pregnancy.

"If you call a one-night stand in the back of his pickup truck love, then yes." She shakes her head at herself.

"Once a farm girl, always a farm girl." I smile at her, testing the waters. She grins back and then breaks out into a full, robust laugh.

"You're funny, Amy. I bet your kids think you're a hoot."

"Oh, you know how it is: no matter how cool the world thinks your mom is, you'll always think she's weird and embarrassing." Her smile fades.

"I would have given anything to get to that stage." Her voice is quiet, and when she looks up at me, I can see the tears forming at the edges again.

"Does your store offer grocery delivery?" I say, looking away so she doesn't know that I see her pain.

"Yeah, we have a runner who does it, not a fancy operation or anything."

"I think I'll need to order some things to deliver to the house I am staying in for the retreat." I get up, walk into the house, search for the bottle of wine I had purchased, and pour myself a glass. "The letter said she only has a small refrigerator, so I think I may run out of creamer. Plus, maybe it's a good idea if someone from the outside world comes and checks on me, you know, just in case this lady is an axe murderer." She didn't follow me into the house, so I am screaming this out to her on the patio. I don't even know if the neighbors are home.

"I'll do it for you," she calls back into the house. "What day do you want them?"

15
Fire

The truths about me are layered and complex. I hold dualities with great reverence, defying all the singular beliefs around the way things need to be. Holding two or more things is not separation, but a coming together. It takes fuel and oxygen for me to burn, one without the other will not produce light.

I am both twenty-nine years old and much, much older. There is a saying that says a flame never dies. We live and burn and when we are done, we keep living. Through old lovers and into revolutions, the sparks we light create change and catalyze lust, love and movement. Our essence floats through the air, becoming one with the exchange of oxygen and carbon monoxide, in and out of lungs, in and out of plants, and back through the air until we are catapulted into the existence of the spark once again.

This iteration of me is twenty-nine years old, but I am only ever as old as when I came in contact with her—the one that my life will always swirl around. I am seven. I am twenty-seven. I am thirty-two. I am twenty-nine. I am older than the Universe.

16
Dr. Lauren

The clock reads 1:44 am. I'm still awake, lying in bed, replaying the scene at Tom's. It is evident to me that my anxiety had taken over, but I don't know what triggered it. Something about being in his house, alone, then in the garden, felt familiar and unnerving. Like a lousy déjà vu that felt exposing and threatening. Going over every detail of his beautifully decorated home and the carefully tended garden left my mind searching for clues but to no avail. Tom didn't say or do anything wrong; if anything, I was rude, acting like an unwelcome guest. I snapped at him, fled the scene, and now must face the music when he delivers the mushrooms. *I could plead the 5th,* I thought, *or blame it on the flame.*

The flame was fine; it always is. Deep down, I knew I would never leave home if there was a chance it would burn out. My anxiety about *the flame* was a desperate chance to control the uncontrollable feeling of vulnerability and intimacy that was in every detail of his life. *It's as if I'd been there before.* I throw the covers off my sweaty body.

I force my mind to travel through a million thoughts, some passing quickly, inviting a welcomed distraction: what I ate for breakfast, if I put too much cream in my coffee, that I haven't seen my squirrel friend in a long time, and how much cleaning I need to do before Amy arrives. These are my everyday, racing thoughts that sometimes occupy me in the middle of the night but usually can lull me back to sleep. But tonight, it's different. My encounter with Tom gnaws at me, bringing up moments from my past that I have tried so hard to forget, but tonight they seem bound and determined for me to deal with them.

I am seven years old and faking sleep in my bed, the light from the hallway shining through the cracked door. I always ask for the light on. My dad complied but turned it off when he went to sleep. I guess adults don't need comfort in the middle of the night.

The sound of their arguing usually lulls me to sleep. Their raised voices reassured me of their presence, and they were also a soundtrack of my childhood. Much like the coffee pot brewing or the rooster crowing, my parents' bickering was a reliable, albeit dysfunctional, source of comfort. That night, I was wearing my dad's polo shirt to bed. Soft and large, the hem went past my knees, and it smelled like him. I tried to fall asleep, but something about their arguing that night made me feel different from all the others. A tone, perhaps, a slight edge found in my mother's voice that was more defiant than the million songs they sang before. My dad responded not in anger but in a quiet, begging modulation that scared me. My dad rose above six feet, always easily picking me up and throwing me over his shoulder in a fit of giggles. He was the first to be there if I fell, the sink pipe burst, or the toilet overflowed. He knew what to do, he never panicked, and everything from the bleeding of my skinned knee to the water that wanted to ruin our bathroom floors obeyed his commands to stop. He was a hero to me, and I knew from watching television and reading my books that heroes never begged. Her voice was threatening; I couldn't make out the words exactly, so I rose and tip-toed to the crack in the door. Cautiously opening it, I knew the creak it would make could not rise above the volume of her screaming. My whole head poked out into the hallway, a risk I was willing to take.

"It's just not working anymore," I heard her say; I didn't need to see her to know her hands were in the air in exasperation.

"What isn't working?" he asked, timid and sad. I thought about his eyes and how, even when he was happy, the corners turned downward, making him seem gentle and innocent, like a puppy. They must be in full force right now.

"Everything. Nothing. I hate my life. If I had known it would turn out like this, I would have never married you. I would have never moved here to this pile of junk and become a mother." She snarled the last word out like it was poison on her tongue.

My breath caught in my chest, my heart began racing, and I felt like hyperventilating. My mother's words cut a deep wound inside of me, and I could feel the blood gushing, threatening to drown every cell in my body. I couldn't breathe.

I don't recall the words he said to her or how long they fought. Time stood still for me as I curled into a ball on the floor of my room, clutching my chest, sweat pouring down my forehead, tears flooding my eyes, wondering if this would be my last breath. This is what drowning must feel like, I thought. I pictured swimming at the community pool and how I knew to hold my breath and make it to the surface before I ran out. "Just make it to the surface, Lauren," I heard the voice say. I pictured the water above me, the disoriented sky that rippled above the surface, and I inched my way to the top. Closer and closer, I rose to the top, my lungs burning and my head dizzy with fear. I could see it now, and just as I broke the water, I gasped a big breath of air, filling my lungs with fresh oxygen. And again. I began to breathe, to recover. I am treading water in the in-between of swimming and surviving, and then I hear the car door slam.

Crawling towards my window, I see my mother backing out of our driveway, her car crammed full of mementos of the life she once lived: high heels, blankets, pillows, her clothes still on the hangers, a curling iron on the dashboard, and her favorite mug on the passenger seat. Still catching my breath, I watched her drive down the street, turning left out of the neighborhood, her tail lights disappearing down the curvy countryside road. I felt like I could vomit.

I stared into the dark, dimly illuminated by staggered street lamps, for what seemed like an eternity until my father's footsteps coming up the stairs snapped me out of my trance. Jumping into bed, I faked sleep as he peered into my room to see if I had heard or seen anything. My closed eyes and now steady breath were convincing enough as he walked down the hallway to his room and got into bed. He left the light on all night that night.

The memory comes flooding back from what seems to be a million years ago, and it hits me as hard as it did the night it happened. It takes over my body, threatening to let the floodgates loose. *She regretted being a mother. She didn't love me, and it was hard to stay.* I think of my seven-year-old self and the trauma this caused me. I think of how this truth has followed me to every relationship, job, friendship, and look in the mirror that I have had since then. I think of how hours of therapy could not undo this tangled mess of rejection and pain that had made a nest inside of me. I think about how, somehow, it has kept me safe because I call the shots now and vowed never to let anyone hurt me again. I think of how it also makes me the most vulnerable; that there is a part of me that will always be that seven-year-old girl in her dad's polo, having her first of many panic attacks as she watches her mother leave, never to return. I think of Amy, who is due here in just a few days, and I think of Tom, who will come in the morning, and I can't afford to feel any of these feelings. And so I do what I don't want: go to *the flame*.

I know she can see me coming and knows what time of night it is. It is the only time I engage in this release of pain and sorrow. I don't want to do it; I try not to do it, but it is the only thing that stops the pain from taking over. I roll up the arm of my sleeve and stare at the flame's light. She is dancing, all the colors in order of blue and yellow and orange and white, and as I inch my arm closer, I feel the heat from the flame reaching towards my already clammy skin. I pause. I think about the Kabbalah class via Zoom I took once and the spiritual explanation for a flame they gave me. I had hoped the class would re-frame *the flame* for me. Maybe it would compel me to see it differently, change the relationship, and stop the pain I put myself through.

The Rabbi who taught the class was kind and elderly, and everything in me wanted to protect him from the outside world. Although it was precisely his experience in the outside world, the pain he had endured and overcome that made him as soft as he was. I watched him talk for an hour, all about the anatomy of the flame, and I marveled at the forgiveness he had in his eyes toward the world, those that hurt him, and himself. He made mistakes, laughed them off; he said the wrong word and didn't even flinch. In one class, his wife walked on camera, and she immediately went on her knees and crawled to get what she needed from the room. He looked straight ahead, assuming none of us could see his wife, army crawling on the ground, so determined to keep things peaceful and intentional.

He explained everything about the flame in terms of consciousness. The wick was the lowest level of consciousness, the thing that most of us consider enlightenment: awareness of the physical body and world. This level of understanding is the most basic form of being alive. Still, we are all so distracted that when we pause long enough to notice the birds singing or the wind blowing, we consider ourselves higher beings.

The next layer of the flame, the one that is usually blue and surrounds the area right around the wick without touching it, is an invitation between our emotions and that which we experience. Its borders are undefined; we hold everything simultaneously here, and this level of acceptance allows it to be so. Here, we can hold joy and grief, pain and healing, sorrow and love. This is the place of the both/and. To be here, he said, we must let our emotions come, feel them, inquire about them, for they will light the way. It is here that I shut down. The feelings are too painful to look at, much less feel. But, if I don't accept the invitation, I can never move on to the next phase of the flame: the outer edge, where we are free.

We all lit a candle at the end of the class and spent time meditating on it. But all I could do was fight the desire to burn myself away. I tried to will it away; I wanted to convince myself I could feel my feelings and look at my pain, but when I stared into that part of *the flame*, all I could remember was that it was the hottest part and how good that would feel on my skin. I signed off the call immediately, not waiting for the class to end, and burned myself again. The class had given me more reasons to scorch my skin: it now felt spiritual, like a death and a sacrifice I was making, like somehow the burning would atone for all my sins. It made it almost imperative that I did it.

Grabbing the candle with my hand, I slowly bring it up to my face. The heat is palpable but also comforting. As soon as it touches my skin, I know it will replace the pain of the past with the smell of burning flesh and give me a wound to tend to. Shaking, I pull the candle closer until I feel the flame singeing my facial hair. This part of the cheek, the lower left corner towards my ear, did not yet have a scar. I take a deep breath, allowing the pain of the past to come to the edge of my consciousness, and right when I picture her face, his body, and that home, I close my eyes and hold *the flame* directly on my skin. I take a deep breath and test myself on how long I can handle the pain before I scream. My record is 20 seconds. *Four one thousand, five one thousand*…each second seems like an eternity. I focus on the agony of the pain and try to bring my mind back to the past.

The memory is fading. *Thirteen one thousand, fourteen one thousand.* I can't handle it anymore, and I yell a tortuous wail from deep within my being. I pull the candle away, and my skin hurts so badly that I can not begin to think of anything else except attending to my wound.

Running to the freezer, I grab an ice pack and put it on my check; I swear I hear it sizzle. *Ah, relief.* Keeping it in place, I head to the medicine cabinet, grab the burn cream calendula salve I got from the market, and put it on the open, oozing wound. I step back and look at my disfigured face in the mirror: the scars are too many to count, a sea of life rafts in an ocean of pain.

I walk back to *the flame.* She sits, dancing again, and I look at her with new eyes, this time of gratitude. She keeps watch over me, protects me from my past, and when we've engaged in our little ritual, she still stands. I keep her alive, and she does the same for me. I pour a glass of wine, put on my favorite Joni Mitchell vinyl, and we do a victory dance together.

17
Jane

There was something about her. How she moved, poured that wine, and overcooked the salmon was endearing. So magnetic. I found myself wanting to confide in her, to ask her for advice. She pried about my life, about this baby, about my doctor, but it didn't bother me the way it usually would. It was kind and caring, like someone with a vested interest in me. Her eyes were soft, her laugh was loud, and she didn't shy away from me and my emotions. I felt held by her. She was this way to me in the bathroom, too. She was sitting next to me, rubbing my back, just a presence until the nausea had passed.

She held a vigil for me, just like the one for Mother Mary I'd attended at the cathedral down the street. I went once for an open prayer service to see what it was like. No one was talking and telling me what to do; all were dressed in robes and using their hands to point at us from a high-up altar. It was just a bunch of quiet people sitting in the pews, some crying, others praying. I just watched. I watched the rows of candles dance among one another, each holding a prayer and a hope that someone lit for someone else they loved. Above the rows of candles was an enormous statue of Mother Mary. I don't know anything about her except that on that day, she was the keeper of the flames. Her arms were open as if to welcome you into her arms, the candles all dancing under her like a brood of baby chicks. The flickering flames, silently chirping, all waiting in a line to cross the great river of life. The day I saw Mother Mary was my mom's birthday, or it would have been.

Her birthday stood out on the calendar my whole life, like the deepest of black holes. It sucked all the energy out of my dad. The solid and reliable farmer who never missed a day of work couldn't get out of bed on my mom's birthday. When I was little, I didn't understand it. He would yell from the other side of the locked door that the chores could wait and there was bread and butter in the fridge. As I grew older, I didn't even talk to him on the fateful day. I managed the animals and made dinner for him, but he did not eat. He never spoke about what he did, alone in his room, and I never asked. I didn't want to know; he was an anomaly that day, and it scared me. I was left to care for myself, to care for our livelihood, and I didn't know if I had lost him for good, too.

In college, I came home on my mom's birthday every year. The first year, I let my dad know, even knocking on his door after I had let myself in. But he never came out, never even acknowledged my presence. I milked the cows, fed the horses, mowed the lawn, and cleaned. I always made a casserole so he'd have something to eat when he came out of his inertia—time stood still that day. I was alone, an orphan for one day a year. No one to hold my grief, forever trapped as a little, 4-year-old girl wandering around the house wondering where my mother and father had gone.

I stopped going home for her birthday once I graduated and moved out. Big Bear wasn't far from my dad's house, but being in the kitchen alone was too painful. I didn't tell him I wasn't coming, and he didn't ask. So that year, determined to have a different day, I walked to the cathedral instead. It felt like something I should do or at least try and do. I have never been the praying type, so I sat in silence and tried to conjure up any memories I had of her. Instead, what came to mind was missing moments of proms, getting my first bra, learning to braid my hair, having my first kiss, and the everyday sense of her. I grieved everything we missed together and also nothing in particular at all. I felt silly to cry over something that never happened, but I couldn't help it. Her absence left a crack in every memory I had as if someone had photoshopped her out of the picture. I feel her absence every day, but in its weird and own way, I also constantly feel her presence. I know she is gone, but I always sense she is still here. Watching and guiding, never really gone but always missing.

I roll over and look at the clock; all these thoughts before 8 am. Rubbing my eyes, I give myself a good stretch with my arms above my head, which reminds me of the subtle changes in my belly. It tightens as I extend, and I put my hand on my womb space. For the first time, I don't feel so afraid. I feel a slight connection between me and this baby, a desire to mother her like Amy had done for me the past few days. I may have a handful of memories of my own mom and me, but it's the intuitive foundation of being mothered that has always been missing. In two small encounters, Amy has given me a taste of what my mother's death took from me.

There is no evidence besides the test that I am pregnant. There are some changes, sure, but I haven't seen her on an ultrasound yet. I can't feel her move, kick, or know exactly what size she is. But she lit a long-lost flame inside me, nestled and protected in my womb. I am the Mother Mary, opening my arms to this possibility. I don't need to see her to know she is here. I feel her warmth glowing, making my body a cathedral of wonder and possibility. *Poppy* would be her name, the flower in the field that lit the whole thing ablaze. In the summer months, when the land was dry and brown, the poppy brought in a burst of color and a reminder that life still lived on. I could feel her embers giving me the gift of instinct I had never fully received. Her flame had lit something inside me, *a mother's intuition,* I think they called it. It was a reckoning of fierce protection of the self, her, and all that lies ahead. To have her in me was to hold vigil for the coming days.

Is it possible that I am considering keeping this baby? Do I dare try to be a mother with no example and no road map in front of me? The thought excites me, but at the same time, it scares me. *But maybe that is what motherhood is always like, walking the line of fear and delight.* I grab my phone, still lying in bed, allowing the morning to enter through my window. Amy was right; I should go to a doctor. That is the logical thing to do. But first, I must tell my dad. Pulling up my list of Favorites, my finger shakily hovers over my dad's picture and name. *Daddy* it says. It hits me that my child will have no one to call by this name. But maybe this baby will at least have a granddaddy. For the sake of this hope, for the baby that I may or may not keep, I allow my finger to descend on the screen, initiating the call.

He answers on the first ring.

"It's my girl!" he bellows. I can hear his smile through the phone and his genuine enjoyment I called. He must be in the barn.

"Hey, Dad," my voice is trembling, but I am confident I am doing an excellent job of faking it.

"What's wrong?" he asks immediately. I have never been able to hide anything from him. It is better not to look him in the eye or talk to his face if I want to keep my inner world a secret. The subject of the call is giving me anxiety, but another layer appears: I don't know how to talk about hard things with my dad. We have never been good at it, so we gave up somewhere along the way, much preferring to sweep things under the rug, never to be discussed again. *I still have no idea how my mom died.*

"I need to tell you something." *Just rip the band-aid off and tell him,* I coach myself.

"Shoot." He says on the other end of the line. I can tell I have his full attention. All the rustling of what I assumed to be barrels of hay being moved has stopped.

I pause. I fight off the feeling of hanging up, to abandon ship, to pretend that I never called. My mouth is suddenly dry, like it's full of cotton, and a lump begins to form in my throat. I know if I don't say it now, I never will. Not telling my dad is not an option. If I skip this step, I know that I will not go through with the pregnancy. Telling my dad at least gives me a chance to decide if I want to, and if I could, be a mother.

"I'm pregnant," I say clearly and as slow as my racing heart will allow. I only wanted to say it once.

He is silent. I wait a few seconds, pull the phone off my ear, and look at the screen to see if he has hung up on me. The call timer is still counting. We've been on the phone for 30 seconds— the only 30 seconds that feels like eight years.

"Oh, sweetheart," he says with a sigh. I can picture him rubbing his brow, his go-to move when deciding what to say.

"Do you want to come home? Have you been taking your meds?" I can't pick up on the tone he is using. It's a mixture of worry and sadness, but the underlying meaning within the modulation around the edges of his words is lost on me. *Exasperation maybe?*

"Did you hear what I said? I'm *pregnant,*" I say again, this time louder and slower.

"I heard you, honey." He soothes me, as he does to the horses when spooked.

"Well, do you have anything to say about it?" My voice is getting louder and more tense. I feel a wave of anger rising within me. He hears me, but he is not listening. Gaslighting, I think they call it.

"I do, I do," he says calmly. "Maybe you can come down here for a few days, and we can spend some time milking the cows or picking daisies. Would you like that?" I can hear his effort to hold back his tears. *Why is he crying? Are these tears of disappointment? What good will it do to go to the farm?*

"Dad, I have a job, and I'm not in a position right now to lose my health insurance." I am no longer trying to control the edge in my voice. My hand grips the phone, my teeth gritted, my cheeks red hot.

He stays calm.

"When was the last time you saw the doctor?" He is not getting it. I want to tell him I am too afraid to go to the doctor alone. I want to say to him that I am terrified of becoming a mother, that the death of mine is still so raw, and the wound has never left me. I want him to know that deep down, I am drowning, and I have been for so long, and I need him right now, more than ever.

"I haven't been," I reply. He sighs a deep, wearied, worn sigh.

"Did you stop taking your medicine?" My doctor had prescribed me anti-depressants a few years prior, and I am pretty faithful about taking them. But I ran out shortly before my one-night stand, and then when I found out I was pregnant, I didn't re-up my prescription.

"Dad," I feel him slipping into the black hole—the same

one from my mother's birthday—the place he goes when things are too tough to face. He is ignoring and gaslighting, turning this around to be about me and what he thinks I should be doing.

"You're the one that should be taking pills!" I scream at him, standing up and pacing around my room. The pressure valve is released, and I let years of pent-up frustration and anger loose.

"You always do this! You leave me when I need you the most. I am going to be a *mother,* and all you can remind me of is how messed up I am." My head begins to throb from the intensity of my screaming. But I don't want to stop.

"I am the way I am because of *you,*" I growl, hot tears streaming down my face.

"Calm down, honey. Can we take a few deep breaths together?" His voice is so quiet and calm it makes me even more angry.

"Dad, no. Not this time. You aren't going to ignore me, make me feel like a piece of shit when I have a chance at happiness. Maybe I'll be a great mother, maybe I'll be the best mother that ever was." I can't stop. The tears are cascading down my cheeks, and the anger won't stop bubbling to the surface.

"I'm sure you would, Jane. I know you would. You will be the best mother." He is so calm, but I hate him. I hate his condescending tone.

"I am not five years old anymore, Dad. I am going to be a *moooottthhhhhher!*" I scream the last word as long as my breath allows, bellowing out the final syllables until my throat hurts. I don't wait for an answer, and instead, I end the call and throw my phone across the room, breaking the full-length mirror on the other side of my bed.

I look and see my reflection in the cracked glass: my belly

has begun to protrude. *It's you and me*, I think. *We will have to do this without him.*

18
Amy

The fancy clubs always had a free phone next to the jacuzzi in the women's locker room. The smell of chlorine, floral shampoo, and liquid body wash that she could never afford, the feeling of air conditioning on the skin. She dialed her parents' number with the white receiver on the wall. 9-4-6-7-1-1-1. When they moved in four years ago, they all laughed that this was the new phone number. It was much more suited for a billboard than a household, but it was nice to know that friends would never forget it. Despite the belief it belonged to a law firm or pizza parlor in its past life, they never received any misplaced phone calls except the one in the middle of the night in which someone on the other end sang the anthem for "Wanting Baby Back Ribs" from Chilis. Ah, the days of the landline.

The busy signal sends a droning cadence into her ear. She hangs up and dials again. She must ask her mother if she can spend the night at her friend's house. Her parents had the membership and her friend's mom, Heather, left the girls to their own devices while she swam, played tennis, and did whatever grown-ups did at an athletic club. She mostly mostly walked around with her friend, pretending they knew how to play tennis or swim laps for hours. She felt like she was in a movie, a feeling that has followed her into adulthood, constantly trying to get back there, to that moment of luxury and freedom. About once a year, she ponders, "Should I join a country club?" She never does.

Until that day, she had never stepped foot in an athletic club. Her family was active, at least mostly; her dad got up every day at 4 am to do a litany of exercises: sit ups followed by push ups and then toe touches. After completing this routine, he set off to run his daily 3 miles. When she got older, she would recall staying in a hotel in upstate New York to take her sister on a college tour and waking up around 4 am only to hear footsteps banging on the floor and excessive panting and breathing. Her dad was running in the corner of the room.

The athletic club boasted of a life of exercise she could not comprehend: the equipment necessary to make it work. She grew up using what was in her yard, her house, and already within her body. She moved her muscles the old-fashioned way. Instead of a stair stepper, she hiked Squaw Peak. Instead of a treadmill, she hit the pavement. If one wanted to lift weights, there were plenty of canned goods. But mostly, it was just running. It's always been running. She watched his body, long and lithe, through the morning dawn as he returned home before sunset. She could hear his heart tick because of a mitral valve put in before she was born. It was faster and louder right after a run and slowed and quieted as his body cooled. He wore the same shorts daily, hanging them out to dry over a lawn chair or from a hanger in the bathroom, sometimes even from the door or window frame. Every week, her mom forced them into the washer, and again, they hung out to dry, only this time on our clothesline; the scent of her childhood: detergent mixed with the smell of sunshine. The feeling of the clothes was a bit stiff from the outside air but softened the moment they touched one's skin. Her friend's mom, Heather, was the opposite. She had outfits at the club. She changed clothes to get onto different machines to make her muscles move. And then, she showered in the middle of the day.

Busy signal. Again. And again. Slamming the phone on the receiver out of annoyance, she tuned into the music on the crackling speaker above. 'Mama said they'll be days like this; they'll be days like this, my mama said!' Singing along, she dialed 9-4-6-7-1-1-1 every few minutes, cursing her sister for using the dial-up internet for such a long time.

She will never forget the blue and red flashing lights that filled her vision when they turned down Laurel Lane—a parade of them together in one clump at the far end of the street. The glow of the red and blue reminded her of Christmas when everyone decorated their front lawns with lights, and they would drive around as a family, slowly, sitting in her dad's lap, her mom and sister in the car, all laughing and singing along to classic Christmas carols on the radio. But, the one-hundred-degree air that came through the car window reminded her that it was not December. As they got closer, the source of the blue and red made themselves clear: a barrage of police cars, ambulances, and fire engines. It did not occur to her that this had anything to do with her until she saw the caution tape that blocked off her street from the rest of the world. And the crowd stared in the same direction, at the same thing. Their mouths hung open as if a scream was caught in their throat, but they just let it sit there, lingering and waiting to release it. She walks up behind the crowd, a bubble of excitement building in her. Nothing happened in their sleepy neighborhood. Following their gaze, she sees it: the shell of something that was once her house—a fire.

The excitement is replaced with dread, a punch in the stomach. Her breath leaves her body. Like the others, she, too, attempted to scream, but her voice caught in her throat, joining in the chorus of horrifying silence. The people in the crowd were the kids at her bus stop and the faces in her classrooms, all staring at her with horror and pity. They knew the house was hers. They had watched it burn. Spotting her father behind the caution tape and breaking the rules, she ducks under the yellow restriction tape, running to him. A policeman stops her, his rough hands grabbing her on the shoulders, "Get back!" he says, sticking out an arm so she can't move any further. Her dad is reaching out to give permission. She runs to him, inhaling her dad's scent on his shirt, but the smell is fleeting. The smell of smoke takes over. The fumes of childhood photos turned to ash, favorite clothes and memories, walls and carpets, all swirling in a million particles around her. If someone had asked her what her life smelled like, she would have answered with her mom's perfume on each wrist and behind her knee for good luck. Or the spice cake and lasagna at every birthday meal. It smelled of her dad's t-shirts she wore to bed or the teddy bear she got in preschool. Never in one million years could she have reduced all of these things to ash, smoke, and soot.

Her sister and mother come to embrace her. The four of them stand, sweaty arms wrapped around each other, tears and beads of sweat rolling down their faces. They watch as the fireman puts out the last of it. The house, barely standing in parts and fallen in others, stares back at their horrified faces—a hollow hole of that which was once called home.

Oh my god. In frustration, I crumple the pages of my journal, which I had just wasted on this "free write." *Oh my god. I suck at writing.* I am heading to Dr. Lauren's this morning, and I (ridiculously) thought if I could write the tale of my house burning down from a third person point of view, it would be out of the way and dealt with before I got there. Lyz has put it in my head that the fire was the ultimate source of all my problems: my anxiety, my lack of creativity, my loneliness…the list goes on. I woke up in the middle of the night last night worrying that I would take the mushroom, and all that would greet me was a diabolical and waxing philosophical diatribe from my psyche about my house burning down. So, I woke up earlier than I wanted, made coffee, and began to write.

I hate writing about things that are real and vulnerable. I much prefer a romance novel or the story of the woman who worked at a marketing firm in New York and then went to help her long-lost boyfriend from her small hometown save his grandmother's bakery! Sighing, I begin to jot down on the fresh page of the paper the thing I am most skilled at: my grocery list.

Jane said she didn't mind bringing me groceries for my integration. I hope that's okay with Dr. Lauren, but I will not ask permission; I will only ask for forgiveness later, if needed. Jane and I had a lovely time together. It felt good to connect with her, and something about her reminded me so much of myself.

It didn't take long for me to realize she needed a mother. My heart ached knowing her mother died so young, and the poetic injustice that this mother was without a mother brought tears to my eyes. I didn't come here to make friends or adopt another child, but I couldn't help myself. Knowing her and her baby's vulnerability made me feel protective. Having her bring me groceries allowed her to think she was doing me a favor, but it also allowed me to check in on her without her feeling smothered.

I make two columns on the list of things I will be bringing:

- Coffee creamer (organic)
- Protein bars
- Fresh fruit
- Tea bags
- Advil
- Bottled water

And the things that I need Jane to bring:

- More coffee creamer (still organic)
- Cabernet (organic)
- Chocolate-covered peanuts (no dyes!)
- Sourdough bread
- Grass-fed butter
- More bottled water

Looking over my list, I am satisfied that my choices reflect the phases and stages of the days ahead: first, fuel up, be ready to be your best self, and then celebrate! Gathering my suitcase, I dump the final drips of coffee in the sink and rinse out my mug. Grabbing my phone, I take a quick picture of my suitcase against the backdrop of my luxurious stay and post it to Instagram: #seeyouontheotherside

Although not recommended, I walk a short distance to the

grocery store. Until now, I have Ubered, but I decided to try it today because it's not even half a mile. I arrive looking unkempt and wishing I hadn't all of a sudden cared so much about getting my steps in. I asked Customer Service if they could hold my bags while I shopped, and I slipped the woman whose name tag read "Sally" a twenty-dollar bill for her trouble. She looked at me with genuine confusion, but there was no protest so I began shopping. I planned to get what I needed and then Uber to Jane's house (she texted me her address—to check up on her, and, of course, give her my grocery list). I thought I'd also throw in a decaf latte and some ginger chews for her.

I find shopping in a new grocery store utterly disorienting. Everything is not where it should be, and the brands are different than I am used to. I head to the dairy section first; a good, quality creamer is arguably the most essential item on the list, and I want to have enough time to scour the shelves for the best option. A glance at my watch tells me I only have 30 minutes to shop if I want to make it to Jane's and then head up the hill to Dr. Lauren's.

The dairy section is much smaller than I am used to, and I quickly eliminate the creamers that I know I won't be buying: anything with high-fructose corn syrup, artificial flavorings, and carrageenan. I don't know why we aren't supposed to consume carrageenan, but a health influencer I follow said not to, and she looks healthy (and skinny!), so I decided to listen to her sage advice. With these options eliminated, I find myself with only five left: all different brands of grass-fed, organic half-and-halves from local(ish) farms. I stare at them for a moment, my body feeling the cold of the refrigerator, and they all look the same. I review them again, hoping to catch something in small print that will make up my mind.

"I'd choose the Cohen Family Farms if I were you," a warm and thick voice interrupts my thoughts from behind me. Spinning around quickly, there is a young man dressed in tight Levi's, a big belt buckle, cowboy boots, and a cowboy hat. He smiles at me and tips his hat. "Hi, Amy," he says as if we have seen one another before.

"I-I'm sorry, but do we know each other?" I ask, stepping aside so the refrigerator door can shut behind me.

"Jane told me about you. I'm Jake, Jake Cohen," he reaches his hand out to shake mine, the other taking his hat off his head and placing it over his heart.

"Ah, from Cohen Family Farms, huh?" I say, shaking his hand and looking at his biased recommendation.

"Yes m'am. The one and only," he seems sheepish, boyish at least. Shy and young, a small-town kid turned adult, taking over the family business.

"Well, I guess I'll take your word for it," I say, opening back up the fridge and moving up to my tiptoes to try and reach the Cohen Family Farms half-n-half that rests on the top of the shelf. *Damn, these heels aren't tall enough.* Jake sees my struggle and reaches right up to grab it for me, placing the glass bottle in my hand.

"We have a recycling program with the grocery store. If you bring the bottle back, you will get $2.00 off your next bottle." That smile again. He is way too young for me (plus I'm married), but certainly not for Jane.

"Are you busy right now, by chance?" I ask, placing the half-n-half in my basket. Feeling the weight against my arm, I wish I had chosen a cart.

"No, ma'am. Today is my day off, and I was actually here looking for Jane. Have you seen her?" He looks around, and I notice that he has a flower in his back pocket.

"Is that for her?" I ask, motioning toward his back pocket.

"Um, yes, ma'am. I noticed she'd been struggling, so I thought this would brighten her day." His face begins to fall as I see him scan the aisles for Jane to no avail.

"I was actually going to stop by to her house today to give her a grocery list. You could take me, instead of an Uber, and then you can give her that flower, too." His face brightens at the suggestion.

"That would be great, Miss Amy," he says, grabbing my basket. He follows me around the store while I get the last few items on my list. It turns out Cohen Family Farms also makes butter and coffee, so I joke that my purchases indirectly pay for his taxi services.

We drive the short distance, mostly in silence, to Jane's house, which is only about five minutes away. I check my watch. If we stay for 15 minutes, I can still make it to Dr. Lauren's on time.

19
Fire

This candle, this post; they do not define me. My life has been much more intimate than that of my ancestors. I am a stolen element from a long line of stolen flames. Humans permanently sealed our fate when they took us from the gods. Once revered and even worshiped, humans only control and contain us, manipulating us for warmth or destruction. Humans do this to us because they do not understand us. Our sparks never fanned into flames outside the body when we were with the gods   and even gods and goddesses ourselves. Our power is *within*. We belong in the womb.

Try and find me within yourself. I'm there, and I always have been. But if you are like her, you have become so good at ignoring me that you've forgotten I am there. If the body were a map, you'd travel six inches below the belly button to find me. I am among many in a complex system, giving life-force energy to the liver, spleen, and gallbladder. I am the second-feeling brain of a human being. While the brain and the head gets tied up in knots of stories you tell yourself, scenarios that have no chance of coming true, I sort it all out.

The center of birth is the safe place where all creation begins: the womb of the soil where the seed securely attaches, the peak of a wave in the ocean before it crashes. It is the space right before everything breaks forth, becoming new again—the seat of the beginning. No one created me; I just *am*. I am *Manipura*. I am intuition.

20
Amy

Okkkkaaaaay. This house is not Instagrammable. The views, maybe, but the house itself looks like a murder happened here, and it's been boarded up ever since. It could be cute; it's an A-frame style harkening back to the 60s, but *damn,* it needs paint, a porch that works, and a massive overtaking of landscaping.

"So this is it?" my Uber driver already has his hand on the reverse gear. "Yeah, I guess it is," I say, climbing out of the car, barely able to shut the door before he speeds away. I would have had Jake take me here, but our pit stop at Jane's never happened due to a flat tire on his truck. While we could have walked, I risked being late to Dr. Lauren's, which was one of my most significant flaws. I Ubered while an apologetic Jake waited for the AAA to rescue him. I have never heard of a farmer who drives into town without a spare tire, but maybe they don't make cowboys the same anymore.

Shifting my weight from one foot to another, I dig in my pocket for the grocery list I never gave Jane. I shoot off the ingredients in a text to her and the address to Dr. Lauren's house. *At least there will be a traceable record of my last contact with humanity,* I think as I pull my suitcase up the worn steps and approach the front door.

I knock twice. I wait. Nothing. "Hello!" I call out, knocking again, this time with so much force; the door opens for me, creaking like a haunted house along the way.

The front room is much more welcoming than the exterior with deep indigo wallpaper covered in flowers and leaves on one entire front room wall. A green velvet couch sits against it, with two white chairs facing it and a coffee table in the middle of the room. *This must be where we integrate.* I am still only peering inside, wondering if I should enter or wait until she greets me. "Hello?" I call again, this time hearing rustling from the other room.

"Amy? Is that you?" her voice beckons from the other room. She sounds cheerful and genuinely happy I am here. I feel my shoulders relax a bit, and my breath becomes steady. I didn't realize my heart was racing, probably (again) because I watch too many horror films. "Yes, it's me!" I call back, pulling myself and my suitcase in the door frame. Hanging plants greet me in giant glass bulbs with macrame slings that stretch to the ceiling. As my eyes adjust, I see a great room beyond the front entrance that expands towards the back of the house, separated by a giant, real-life tree trunk.

"Come in! I'll be right out," her voice sounds sing-songy like Sleeping Beauty surrounded by birds and bunnies is about to greet me. I walk towards the tree and can fully see into the room beyond. The room is covered with velvet pillows and blankets and looks like a den of safety and warmth, with a splash of hippie for good measure. An altar with objects ready for our ceremony sits under one of the many windows covering the wall's length, and a blank canvas with a dozen tubes of oil paints and a cup of paintbrushes sits near the tree in the center of the room. The pine trees are on display behind it, and the scenery is the most beautiful and breathtaking I have ever seen. I grab my phone to try and take a quick picture so that I can remember it forever. And, of course, post it later.

"I'm sorry, I have a strict 'no picture' policy. You understand, don't you?" She is standing behind me and has caught me red-handed. Embarrassed, I quickly shut off my phone (before sneaking a picture, of course!) and quickly turn to meet her. Instead of Sleeping Beauty, an aged, gray, witchy-haired woman stares back at me. Her clothes are large layers covering her body, making it almost impossible to know what shape her body is. She is wearing browns and tans, a ring on every finger, and a colorful scarf adorns her neck. But what is most surprising about her are the scars that adorn almost every inch of her face.

I gasp despite myself, my hand flying up to my mouth as if I have just witnessed a tragedy, and I immediately feel horrible for doing so. I can't help it—she is the complete opposite of what I expected her to be, and it's taking me by complete surprise. I don't mean to sound shallow but thank God *there is a no-picture policy. There are no amount of filters to help her face.*

"I'm sorry," I whisper, the color leaving my face. "That was incredibly rude of me. I'm Amy, and it's very nice to meet you." I approach her, worried that she will tell me to leave, but I stick out my hand.

"It's nice to meet you too. Sorry, I wasn't there to greet you. I have a cat named Theo, and I was making sure he was all set before we started." If she was offended by my reaction, she doesn't show it. Her hand is warm and soft; she must moisturize. She smells of jasmine and violets with a hint of vanilla. *I would have put her more in the patchouli family. This woman is full of surprises.* As I look at her face more closely, curiosity arises in me. *These are prescribed burns, not a childhood accident.* I know due to my aforementioned watching of horror and true crime films. But before I can hypothesize, she expertly turns the attention back to me. *This is not her first rodeo.*

"Why don't you put your bag in the guest room right down the hall, and we can get started. Did you follow the recommendations of not eating anything this morning?" She is walking towards the kitchen, and I nod. "I sure did!." I spoke too cheerfully. I am an awkward liar. I did not follow the directions because I did not read the directions. This is also why I didn't know about the "no picture policy." I curse myself for never reading the pamphlets, the instructions, and the forwards. I make a mental note to go to the bathroom and skim the PDF she sent me before I begin the process.

"Oh, and you can turn off your cell phone and put it here," she says, pointing to a basket on the kitchen counter.

"Can I just make one last call?" I say nervously. I don't know what I expected, but I have never been without my phone for a full day, much less a full day with a witch stranger who is about to give me drugs.

"No need. This house is a dead zone. I did that on purpose. Too many people get distracted by modern technology when we are here to do important work." *Is that a look of revenge?* I look down at my screen, and sure enough, SOS is written in the top right corner where my antenna bars usually reside. *SOS is right.* I walk over to the basket, powering my phone off along the way, and I am so glad that Jane will be coming tomorrow with the groceries. I won't fully unpack in case I need to make a getaway.

"Of course," I say, dropping my phone in the basket and heading to the guest bedroom with my suitcase. It is as plain but as beautiful as they come. A queen bed with a white puffy comforter sits in the middle of a small bedroom with walls with hand-painted, yellow daisies. A chandelier hangs from the ceiling, and a little armoire with a mirror and a place for me to put my makeup sits in the corner of the room. Right next to each side of the bed are two nightstands, one with magazines about Big Bear and, of course, psychedelics, and the other has a basket with a few items for me during my stay: a bottled water, hand towel, facial moisturizer, chewing gum, and an eye mask to wear during sleep. *What a nice touch.*

I take a few minutes to get out my essentials, use the restroom, and contemplate whether I should brush my teeth before I take the mushrooms. Deciding it may alter the taste, I rinse my mouth with water instead. Taking one last look in the mirror, I admire my sequin jumpsuit again and return to the living room.

Dr. Lauren has arranged all the pillows into a circle on the main room's floor as if we are expecting multiple visitors. The blankets have been piled atop a small foam mattress in the middle of the circle with a pillow for someone to rest their head. *I will be that someone.* As if she can sense my hesitancy, she says, "It's only us, and I find that once the medicine takes over, clients do best lying down." She pats the pillow beside her, right before the altar. I take my seat. The sequins on this jumper are itching me a little, but I know wearing them will be worth the discomfort.

"Do you have any questions before we begin? Maybe there was something unclear in the packet I sent over?" She is sitting cross-legged, her hands resting on her knees and her eyes locked with mine. *Creepy, right?*

"No! I'm all good! Good, good, good!" I give her a thumbs up. *What the fuck?*

"Ok then, let's get started." She rises to her feet and offers a hand to help me. Together, we face the altar that she has prepared for our session. She begins by clanging the sound bowl, directing me to inhale and exhale deeply. I silently thank my meditation app for preparing me for this moment. The first time all day, I didn't look like a fool. *I am a professional breather, and it shows.* Once the tone has played out, she directs me to open my eyes and explain the significance behind every object on the altar. The turkey feather represents the ancient cultures that owned the land and taught us the ways of plant medicine. The fresh flowers represent all that is alive in us and around us, while the small bowl of water represents the tears of grief that we have cried. And finally, the candle is the flame burning in us and protecting us, something she has lit for twenty-nine years.

"Wait, twenty-nine years?!" My semi-shriek breaks the silence like a bull in a china shop. "Are you fucking serious?" She stifles a laugh, breaking her very serious-medicine-woman facade.

"What is twenty-nine years to you, Amy?" She asks, looking at me intently once again.

"No, I mean, how in the world have you kept it alive? Do you not leave the house?" Again, my foot is in my mouth, but *isn't that a fire hazard?*

"I have my ways of keeping it safe. But to answer your question, I live a straightforward and slow life." Her tone tells me we are done with this topic, but my mind has difficulty leaving it. *A candle that has been burning for twenty-nine years? That means it started when I was 11 years old. I was a child, full of wonder and sunshine, my whole life ahead of me, when she was at this house, lighting that thing, sealing in her fate.* A feeling of sadness flushes over me as I picture her, probably in her early thirties, coming here and deciding this was where she would stay. Suddenly, the scars make a little more sense. I know she is a therapist, but it doesn't take a doctor's degree to understand what all signs here point to: a life of hurt and pain. *Maybe she is the subject of my next book; I could-*

"Do you understand?" She interrupts my thoughts. *Understand what? Ugh. I missed another set of instructions.* Bravely, I stammer, "I'm sorry, I got distracted. Can you repeat that?" She takes a small breath and patiently repeats

herself: "The candle is never to be blown out. It stays
lit. Therefore, I am the only one who holds, moves, or touches
it. Is that clear?"

"Yes, ma'am. I won't get near the candle." *Will I remember
these details after the mushroom? I sure as hell hope so.*
"Ok, then we are ready for the psilocybin. I have two choices for
you. Both are psychedelics, although scientifically, they are
different mushrooms. I can't choose which is best, only you can
decide. We sit back down on our round, velvet cushions and
face one another, both sitting crossed-legged, our knees
touching. In her left hand is exactly what I thought it would look
like: a medium-sized brown and white mushroom with a little
cap and a stem. *I really, really wish I had my phone.* In her right
hand is a small square piece of chocolate. *That's not at all what I
was expecting.*

"How do I know which one to choose?" I ask, looking back
and forth between the two.

"I want you to hold each one, feeling its vibration in your
hand, allowing its energy to connect with yours," she says,
handing me the brown and white mushroom first.

This mushroom is what I expected to consume and the most
authentic choice for the occasion. It is soft, almost velvety, and
lightweight. *Less calories.* But it in't glamorous or fun; it is a
fungus. I sit, holding it, with my eyes closed, trying to connect
my energy with its energy or whatever the fuck she said. *Any
minute now, I'll feel it.* But nothing. I open my eyes and smile
slightly, nodding, pretending I knew what I was supposed to
feel. Handing the mushroom back to her, I am eager to hold the
chocolate.

It feels like a regular piece of Hershey's, maybe slightly less
heavy. It is smooth and smells delicious, and a helluva lot more
Instagrammable than the mushroom—a *better story to tell later.*

But still, I sit with my eyes closed and will my hand to tingle as our energies connect, but nothing. I open my eyes again and nod at Dr. Lauren. It is unclear if she knows that I felt nothing.

"Hold one in each hand, and your body will tell you which one it needs. Whichever one feels the heaviest, that is the one your body wants."

Finally, some clear direction on this. I sit, my back fully erect, as I learned in yoga, allowing my hands to rest openly on my knees. I hold the mushroom in my left palm and the chocolate in my right.

I raise them slightly above my knees, very skeptical that I will feel anything, and for the millionth surprise today, I am shocked to experience my left hand feeling heavy, like there is a brick in it, while the right feels like I'm holding a feather. I open one eye to see if it looks heavier or just feels that way to me. Both hands look equal, like a balanced scale. *The mushroom is heavier. The mushroom is what your body needs.* I sit with my eyes closed and desperately try not to assign meaning to this. Lyz says that I make up narratives about what something means when those stories aren't real. My story is that I am average, ordinary, and boring. The mushroom reserves itself for people like me; thus, my trip will be average, ordinary, and boring. I open my eyes ever so slightly. *Can she tell which one is heavier?* I see her, barely, sitting with her eyes closed as well. *Has she fallen asleep?*

She breaks the silence. "Does one feel noticeably heavier to you, Amy? Trust your body." Ha! *There's a phrase.* I haven't been able to trust my body since the day I was five, and looked in the mirror at the Disney store wearing a Beauty and the Beast princess dress, crying because I though I was fat. I haven't trusted my body since it strangled my baby when it was supposed to keep him safe. I haven't trusted my body since no matter what I feed it or don't, exercise or rest, drink or not, it just keeps getting bigger. *Maybe the key is doing the opposite of what my body tells me to do.*

"Yes, yes, I do," I say quietly, resting my hands on my knees.

"Excellent," she says, and I can tell she is smiling. Let's open our eyes." We make eye contact again, and I am getting used to her scars.

"Which one does your body need, Amy?" She puts her hands out in front of me so I can hand her the one my body doesn't need. And I pause.

I am not in the practice of listening to my body. In fact, for many years, I have ignored her, pushing down every urge and desire, everything that may feel good. I have difficulty knowing if I am hungry, thirsty, or need a nap. I have never masturbated, and orgasms are hard for me to relax into; I always stop them before they're fully realized. I want desperately to trust her, and a profound thought enters my mind: *maybe this is part of the journey. What if you trusted your body, ate the mushroom, and had the most profound experience of your life?* I feel myself responding with gratitude, a small tremble, the start of tears, and a small feeling of warmth inside my gut. *Is that my intuition? I haven't heard from her, well, ever.* I sit with her for a moment, closing my eyes again, picturing the flame on the altar sitting inside me now. *Could this be my moment? That I come to this house and light a new light that guides me for the next twenty-nine years? What would it be like to listen to myself, trust what I need, and know what I want?* I pull my hands off my knees again, testing the felt-weight one last time. My right hand holding the chocolate feels like air, while the mushroom's weight is almost too much—the flame in my gut flickers. *Take the mushroom,* it says.

And then.

I hear the story again about being neutral and bland. I feel the scratch of my sequin jumpsuit on my forearms, and I remember why I am here: I am not here to learn to trust myself. I am here to have a creative breakthrough, to become a famous author, and to tell the story later. There was plenty of time to trust my body later. Maybe when I'm done with my book, I'll do more yoga. The chocolate represents everything I want in my life and have wanted but never had: a unique and sexy story that fast-tracks me to where I want to be. The chocolate may not be heavy, but I can't ignore the track record of untrustworthiness my body has had.

"My body needs the chocolate." I hand over the mushroom, and before I change my mind, I pop the chocolate into my mouth. *Let the journey begin.*

21
Dr. Lauren

I hear her car pull up and I duck down under the window so I can sneak a peek at her before she sees me. It takes her a minute to get out of the car, although the driver's reverse lights are on the second he pulls up. Even though the lack of curb appeal is by design, his obvious hurry to flee stings a little. The witchy-aesthetic is the first test of the retreat. No one has ever walked away, but I can tell a lot about a person by the way they react when they see where I live. I study her face closely as she exits the car, but my eyes are immediately diverted due to head to toe sequins sparkling in the sun. I can't help but laugh. *No way!*

I have never had a client *dress up* to take mushrooms. Upon closer look, I see her hair is perfectly curled, and hanging loosely by her shoulders. It frames her face which is slender and somehow she learned the "natural beauty" look which actually uses far more makeup than I have ever owned. This can not be the same person as the picture she sent in: messy, unkempt, not put together. This woman, standing in a sequin jumpsuit with silver, 5-inch heels and circle Chanel sunglasses is none of these things. *Shit. Shit. Shit.* My cheeks grow hot and I begin to sweat in the tan cotton shirt I got from the co-op five years ago. I am suddenly embarrassed by everything my life has turned out to be. The secluded and simple life I have chosen, a grasp at superiority in a world of shallowness and image-obsession. I have routinely convinced myself that *inner beauty* was the most important thing and have neglected myself again and again for the sake of the upper-hand. But who have I been trying to beat? Not the men in suits or boat shoes that walk through my door, and certainly not the glamor girl Amy who, in a matter of moments, will walk through my door and see all of my flaws and scars. I made myself look exactly how I feel; ugly and unlovable. *Inner beauty, my ass.*

I jump up and run to my bedroom, located behind the kitchen and pray her suitcase gets stuck in the rocks giving me a few extra minutes. Frantically, I leaf through my closet to find something suitable, not sequined, but suitable. Everything I own looks like it came off the bargain table at goodwill, and it all smells musty and moldy, too.

"Hello?" I hear her yell from the other room. *Shit. Shit. Shit.* I peel off my shirt to reveal my bra that is hanging on by a thread, my squishy and *very pale* stomach that is flopping over the sides of my elastic waistband. I grab the least offensive top from my hangers and wrap a scarf from the bottom of my drawer loosely around my neck. I don't own any perfume, but grab some Febreeze from under my sink and swirl the aerosol around me. Shoving it back into the cupboard, I stop and look at myself in the mirror. *Not amazing, but better.* Until I see my face.

"Hello? Dr. Lauren?" She is calling again, this time her voice ringing closer. She must have let herself in.

"Amy? Is that you?" I raise the pitch of my naturally low and growly voice to sound chipper and welcoming.

"Yes! It's me!" She says, the glitter from her jumpsuit must have seeped into her veins, her voice sounds like a cold glass of Rosé.

"Come on in! I'll be right out!" I call, attempting to match pitch. I've seen my face a million times. Usually, I have a sense of pride about all that I have endured. I give myself grace for burning my own flesh as I know, deep down, it's a reflection of the pain I have survived But today, as I gaze at myself in the mirror, all I see is the stark contrast of Amy's flawless face. I consider attempting to cover my skin up with makeup but curse myself for not owning any. Searching the drawers for cream or any type of concealer, I regret buying into the herbal face wash with no chemicals and the belief the ladies down at the market sold to me that, "skin health is what you put *in* your body and not on it." *Fuck that.*

I emerge from my room just in time to see Amy, standing in my living room with a picture perfect aura around her. *Her shit probably smells like flowers.* I am so enamored by her delicate and celebrity-like appearance that I almost miss the fact she is pulling out her phone to take a picture of my living room.

"I'm sorry, I have a strict 'no picture' policy. You understand, don't you?" I say, breaking the silence. I hold my breath as she turns and sees my face for the first time. I briefly wonder if she has been warned, but judging by her reaction, it is clear she has not. Her hand flies to her mouth as an audible gasp escapes. *She is horrified.* Her eyes, as big as saucers, look me up and down and land on my distorted face. I meet them, searching her surprised expression for whatever feeling lies beneath. *Embarrassment.* She owns up to her reaction, sticks out her hand, and our palms meet.

Her skin feels as smooth as it looks; and when our hands touch I feel an electric pulse between them. I see it now, the look in her eyes that I saw in the photo. *Joy.* It's there, behind the beauty and the makeup and the sequins, *joy* lurks below the surface. *I am undone.* Tears begin to form, I feel the fist in my throat, and it's all I can do to change the subject. Directing her to the guest room, I vow to make quick work of the introduction to the process and get the psilocybin into her mouth as quickly as possible.

The altar I have in the ceremony room has sacred items I have received along my own journey to be a psilocybin guide. Normally, I take my time, going through each one ceremoniously, explaining them, allowing my clients to become oriented to their presence. But I can't today. For the sake of self preservation, I need her to stop looking at me and instead, start looking at herself. I need space where she will be in her own world, so I can figure out how to be in mine again. I need the version of her, the Amy that walked in the room, the one who is put together and joyful and gorgeous, to be exposed and made vulnerable. I need to see her weakness so I don't feel so bad about mine.

Sitting down on one of the round cushions, I glance at *the flame.* She is still there, still burning, ready to honor whatever happens next. Her heat flirts with the skin on my face, telling me she will bring relief. I have never burned when a client is here, even though I know I could get away with it. But today, the temptation feels strong. And yet, I find myself not wanting to add another scar to my already hideous looking face.

She enters the room and takes a seat among the cushions. I rattle through a few formalities asking if she has any questions. I know she hasn't read the packet I sent over or she wouldn't have tried to take a picture. I get right to the point, pulling down the two choices of mushrooms I have for her. Immediately, I regret giving her a choice.

The usual fare is a plain looking, obvious mushroom. There is nothing glamorous about it and is always what everyone expects. Men seem to like this mushroom; biting off a raw fungus ignites a primal force in them, as if they might break out of their business suit and reveal a mountain man cape and superhero suit underneath. But Tom stopped by early this morning with a piece of chocolate. He dried two different types of mushroom and then ground them to a fine powder. From there, he mixed it with melted dark chocolate and poured it all into a mold. It was completely unnecessary and totally sophisticated. And it was perfect for Amy.

I shudder thinking of the awkward interaction with Tom. I still haven't recovered from the last time I saw him, but instead of owning up to my mistake, I acted like nothing happened. He was taken off guard and tried to apologize himself, but I cut him off and grabbed the chocolate from him, making an excuse that Amy would arrive any minute. I honestly didn't even catch what mushrooms he used. *Good thing I trust him.* I would love to patch things up with him, and *I will*, I promised myself. I didn't realize how much I enjoyed his company, even the little we interacted, until it threatened to not be available anymore.

I gave Amy the choice between the mushroom and the chocolate. I immediately can tell she is enamored with the elegance and sexiness of the latter. I don't blame her. Even I was tempted to take a close up picture of her perfectly straight, white teeth biting into the chocolate, her perfect red-lip resting on its glossy, dark surface. My hope is that she will choose with her heart not her Instagram filter.

I learned in my training that the body always knows. If you can get in touch, even barely, your body will tell you what it needs. The easiest way to do this is by feeling the weight of a substance in your hand. If your body needs it, it will feel heavy; if your body doesn't need it, it will feel light as a feather. I tell Amy these instructions and she nods politely, taking me and the process seriously. I appreciate her earnest search as she closes her eyes and attempts to feel the weight of each substance.

Immediately, the hand with the mushroom falls closer to her knees. *Trust the process.* She evens them out, but I can tell from here which one her body needs. I sit with my eyes closed, waiting for her to come to her intuitive choice. This, perhaps more than the trip itself, is an integral part of the process. If she goes against her intuition, the whole trip will be harder than it needs to be. The thing about mushrooms is that they work *with* the person so if the person isn't showing up authentically, there are more layers to unpeel on the front end of the trip.

The silence is longer than I expect it to be, and I find myself impatient. I want desperately to get past this stage. Opening my eyes a slit, I see her doing the same. I can't be sure what she is thinking, but I know from experience it shouldn't take this long to know which one is heavier.

"Does one feel noticeably heavier to you, Amy? Trust your body." I try to hurry her along.

"Yes, yes it does." She answers. *Finally.*

"Which one does your body need?" I probe. And she still sits. She waits. As if she is deciding to tell the truth or not. I see the mundane in conflict with the glamor and I remember her application. *A bored housewife who wants to win a Pulitzer Prize.* She has a medallion she's holding on to, certainly a product of "manifesting" or whatever the hell they call it. The brain certainly does work in neuropathic ways. The cellular network is constantly listening, and studies have proven that what we say can actually change our biology. But manifesting relies on the idea that what we say will change the Universe. I admit I haven't dabbled in it as an effort to understand it as much as I could have because the whole thing feels like a crock of shit. I can repeat my desires as many times as I want, and my body may in fact feel like it has achieved them, but it doesn't mean it actually has. Manifesting, I have surmised, leads to delusion.

I open my eyes and take a moment to try and really see Amy. If I can put on my therapist hat for a moment, I have a chance at finding empathy and understanding for her. More will be uncovered once the mushrooms do their magic, but if I could guess, she has repeated a mantra about winning the Pulitzer so many times that her body believes she will. If her body believes it, then her brain will continually make choices that it feels align her with this action, even when they make no sense. Why? Because she also has a prescribed idea of what it means to win a Pulitzer, or more likely *who* is the type of person that wins one. As she stares at the mushroom in one hand and the chocolate in the other, I see myself in her. I, too, am a product of creating my own reality no matter the cost.

I see her gaze soften and her shoulders relax. Her perfectly straight spine gives a little, and I imagine her flat abs are forced to surrender under her jumpsuit. Just as I think she is going to pick the mushroom, she presses fast forward on her psyche, and practically throwing the mushroom back into my hand, shoves the piece of chocolate in her mouth.

There is a hint of rebellion and satisfaction, and even a little regret. Her mouth begins to chew furiously and I can't hide my shock. It is my turn to gasp and allow my hands to fly to my mouth. *Either I was wrong, or she betrayed her own body.* My palms begin to sweat and I nervously watch her chew the piece of chocolate, her jaw moving up and down like it's tar. *I should have listened to Tom. Were there special instructions?* It's too late to phone a friend, and so I surrender myself to whatever will unfold.

22
Jane

My first appointment is with the doctor. Her office looks like an episode of *The Golden Girls*, with mauve and fake flowers strewn about. The scent is "air freshener." The chairs, covered in a dusty, pink velvet, creak when I take a seat, the cream and gold wallpaper witnessing it all. Framed photos cover the walls, all photographs of babies in non-baby costumes, like sunflowers, peas in a pod, and a newborn laying across a pumpkin with the vines coming out its back. *Totally creepy.* I want to text Amy or Sally a photo of these as a joke, but I stop myself short. *This has to be just me.*

I didn't tell anyone I was coming here. Amy and Sally would have offered to accompany me, but I knew I needed to experience this visit and her heartbeat all on my own. As I wait in the room, full of other pregnant mothers whose bellies are already showing, I adjust the flower crown on my head. It is the one skill, besides milking a cow, that my mother passed down to me.

I still hadn't spoken to my dad since the day I told him I was pregnant. It killed me, being hurt by him. It wasn't just that he didn't believe me; he never has. A large portion of my experience is people, my dad specifically, not believing me. I think back to the million words left unsaid between us over the years, the things I saw and learned that he saw and learned differently, and how there wasn't space for both of us. The more I accepted this, the further he retreated, leaving days and weeks of silence and pleasantries passing through us and forcing me to dig a hole and bury what hurt and needed healing. It was always then that the poppies showed up. We would argue about crayons and then curfews, disagree on politics or future possibilities, or have to face my mom's birthday or death anniversary. A poppy would appear on my pillow, in a little vase on the table, or on the dashboard. Just one at a time, a constant sprinkling of apologies and hugs that he could never give in person.

So it was no surprise that today, when I opened my door to let the morning air in, a big bouquet of fresh poppies awaited me. There was no note to accompany it, no text message or call saying he was there, just the poppies with a rubber band around the stems, lying on my welcome mat adorned with a blue butterfly. Upon seeing them, I did the only thing I knew to do: make a crown. *This is how my mother will come with me to my appointment.*

I made my first flower crown with her help when I was around five. My coordination was barely able to get the twists just correctly. Mama was patient, encouraging me the whole time, and never let me give up. "You start with any three stems you want," she said that day, holding up three poppies with a big smile.

"Each one should represent something you want in your life. I want health, happiness, and cookies," she giggled. She touched the tip of my nose with the poppy's bright yellow and orange flower.

"Me too!" I said with glee. *I should have wished to have her forever;* I grieve now, feeling the intertwined stems placed delicately on my head. The stems, braided together expertly, end to end, the new braids feeding into one another until they all hold tightly, were said to keep our hopes and wishes. Mama and I made these so much it was the closest thing to a prayer I knew. The year she died was also the year of the superbloom. Visitors from all over came to Redlands on their spring breaks to see it, and Mama and I made thirty crowns and sold them on the side of the road for $2 each. She took me to get a hot fudge sundae with our earnings.

Instead of three intentions, I assigned each stem to my baby, Mama, and me. I wrapped up everything I loved about her that I hoped for myself and wondered about Poppy repeatedly until the crown was full of love and wonder, with some grief and fear sprinkled in. I knew it was all a part of the cycle, the light and the dark. In the year of the superbloom, Mama said we were the luckiest ones.

"Because we get to see the flowers every year?" My wide eyes were curious as she tucked me into bed that night.

"Because we see them when they are just sprouting until they die. Resurrection, every year, all around us." She kissed me on the forehead, something I can still feel when I conjure it each night.

Today, my crown is a little resurrection: death, life, and the in-between embodied in a tangle of wildflowers atop my head.

"Jane?" The nurse props the door open with her hips, clipboard in hand, calling my name. *This is it.* I get up, waving shyly but proudly, and follow her to the back of the office.

"When was your last period?" the nurse practitioner asks, laptop at the ready. I count in my head when I had received a positive pregnancy test and then walk it back about a month.

"Around six or maybe eight weeks ago? Whenever that was." I am embarrassed that I don't know for sure. I look down at my hands, afraid she is keeping notes about things like this because the small things always add up to be the big things. I fear this is a marker that gives a clue about a person forgetting their child's birthday or the first day of school.

"No problem. We will get a good look at the baby and measure exactly how far along you are. From there, we can give you a due date. Mmmkay?"

"Yes, ma'am," I say, although I think we are the same age.

"Because you are early in your pregnancy, we will do a transvaginal ultrasound. Later on, we will do the abdominal one." I nod as if I have any clue what she is talking about. She continues talking, handing me a hospital gown that has been neatly folded, "I'm going to step out; if you can undress from the waist down and put on this hospital gown, I will be right back, and we can start the ultrasound." She walks out, closing the door behind her. The silence I am left with is deafening. I am in a moment of no return. What happens next will be a huge factor in deciding whether I want to keep this baby. I read online that people suggest *not* listening to the heartbeat, but I know myself. I need every ounce of information before I can choose.

I undo the hair tie I have used to button the top button of my pants and pull them off my hips until they are in a pile at the bottom of my feet. *Should I leave my socks on?* I pull my underwear off and take my socks with it, allowing my feet to touch the cold, tiled floor. Although I am now standing in the middle of the office, half naked, I take a moment to fold my jeans nicely, tucking my underwear and socks in between the folds. I don't know why, but I feel embarrassed about her seeing my underwear. Hopping back on the table, I cover my lower half in the hospital gown and lie on my back, staring at the ceiling and remembering to breathe.

"Are you ready?" she says on her way into the room. *Here we go.* "Yes," I choke out in a whisper, barely able to hear my own words.

"Go ahead and scoot to the bottom of the table and put your feet in these stirrups. Just like you would at your annual.' *Annual?* I scoot down to where she is standing until I feel my butt on the edge of the table and put my feet in the stirrups on each side. I feel so vulnerable. Holding up a long wand-looking device, she puts a condom on it and then rubs lubricant on it. *This looks familiar,* I can't help but giggle.

"I'm going to put this inside you gently, and it will give us a clear picture of the baby. I will go slow, but please tell me if it hurts." She lifts the gown and places the wand inside me with expert gentleness and precision. Her eyes are on the screen, and while one hand holds the wand, the other punches numbers on the ultrasound keyboard. *She is better at this than he was.* Maybe it was the booze or the bed truck, but this nurse handled the wand better than the boy who got me here.

Black-and-white images splash across the screen as the tech moves the wand around and around in circles, her eyes searching the screen. She occasionally clicks the keyboard, punching in numbers that I can't understand.

"Let's see, sometimes, the baby hides," her hand veering very much to the right.

"Ouch," I wince.

"I'm so sorry, Jane. I am trying to find the baby, I don't want to hurt you, so let's try the abdominal ultrasound." *She can't find the baby.* My mouth is dry, my heart is racing, and I can feel the panic begin to set in.

"If you could just scoot back up the table so your head is on this pillow," she fluffs it like a maid in a nice hotel. I do as she says, my vagina wet and gooey, wondering how I will wipe it all off. She gently pulls the hospital gown off my shoulders, exposing my bralette until my stomach is bare. Squirting more goop on my belly, she straightens up a bit taller, clearing her throat and smiling.

"Let's try this again." *She is feigning confidence.* Again, she goes about her job with poise and expertise, one hand moving a new wand in slow circles on my belly and the other typing things on a screen. But she says nothing. I say nothing. I glance from her to the screen and back again, hoping I can figure out what she sees based on her facial expression. She keeps a poker face.

After a moment of excruciating silence, she returns the wand to its holder near the computer and gently touches my arm.

"I'll be right back, Jane; I'm going to get the doctor." I nod and smile, but I don't know why. I am terrified. *Maybe this is what I need to know, and I want to keep her. This fear that something is wrong may be the answer you're looking for.* I try to comfort myself. I lay there on my back, my stomach and vagina covered in goop, and I stare at the wood-paneled ceiling above me. I search the dark lines of the wood to find shapes and animals, as I did when I was little. I can locate an avocado pit, a unicorn horn, and, most importantly, a heart.

"Hi Jane," she enters without knocking, the nurse following close behind her. "My name is Dr. Kong, and I'm going to take a look at things, okay?"

"Ok, nice to meet you." I swallow all my fears and questions and wait as she repeats the same process. The nurse and I just went through, with more goop, the camera wands circling, and the click of her fake nails typing on the computer. I watch her eyes scan the screen. The nurse points out something that is gone as fast as it is there, and the doctor mumbles something I can't hear. She keeps her eyes on the screen but asks me a series of questions:

> "When was your last period?"
> "When did you take a pregnancy test?"
> "Have you had any bleeding since then?"

I answer her to the best of my ability even though I increasingly feel the urge to vomit. She stops searching with the wands and wipes my stomach with a clump of Kleenex next to her.

"Jane." She is looking at me with confusion, and I don't understand. *What is there to be confused about?* "Both my nurse and I have looked, and we can't find anything on the ultrasound." Her hand is on my arm, gentle and reassuring.

"You mean there is no heartbeat?" I say, aware that this means I will miscarry the baby in the next few days.

"Usually, if there is no heartbeat, and you haven't already miscarried the baby, we see an embryo or a sac in the uterus. That's how we know that there was a baby there but that the baby hasn't survived. However, there is no embryo in this case, as if you were never pregnant." A familiar look of pity, not remorse, forms on her face. *She feels sorry for me?*

"I don't understand. The test I took it-" my voice wanders off, my breathing becomes heavy, and the room begins to spin.

"We tested your urine today, too, and three tests came up negative." She looks at me like she has caught me.

"Do you think I made it up? I saw the pink lines! I have had morning sickness and cravings, too!" I get up as fast as I can, almost falling over as I put my clothes back on as fast I can. I hear Dr. Kong trying to calm me down, "No one thinks you made it up, Jane. Maybe your hormones are off, and we can do blood work to determine the issue."

"The tests say you can get a false negative but not a false positive!" I scream, tears streaming down my face.

"Tests, unfortunately, aren't perfect. Everything has a margin of error." She places her hand on my shoulder again, and I shake it off immediately.

"You're wrong! What about the margin of error in *your* office?" I point my finger at her out of rage, grief, and confusion. *She doesn't believe me, just like my dad.* The only person who has believed me is Amy. She never asked for proof; she never questioned Poppy or me. She was simply there for me.

Dr. Kong is reviewing my chart now, asking about vitamins I may be taking, and she lands on the medication list. "Are you still taking the bipolar medicine?" *Gaslighting is what they call it.* I feel myself slipping back into my cave—where I grew up, the one I should have never left. The cave keeps me safe. The cave believes me.

Mortified, I dig down to a deep place of embarrassment stored inside me. I find the many times I became skilled in ignoring pity from the people in my town; I summon a small act of courage: I don't owe her an answer; she is not my mother; she is nothing to me. I keep my mouth shut, quickly get dressed, grab my purse, and storm out the door, slamming it behind me. Running out of the building as fast as I can, I don't stop until I sit in my car's front seat. Taking a few deep breaths, I recall I have a Planned Parenthood appointment in thirty minutes. Seeing another set of doctors is the last thing I want to do. *I need to see Amy.* She believes me. I am not supposed to bring her groceries until tomorrow, but the need to see her feels desperate, as if my life, no my baby's life, depends on it.

23
Fire

"A fire is an event or occurrence, not a thing."

This is what the books and my ancestors say. A chemical process in which certain, scientific things must happen to make us alive. A million moveable parts that must fall exactly in the right place at the right time. AND. We are not *only* this. The process is what brings me to life and back to life again. It is the journey, the reincarnation of the self, becoming a new thing with parts from our past lives each and every time.

When the process is complete, we are most certainly *things*. But what if the process can't be completed? What if there is one element missing? Do we ever sporadically, against all odds, fan into flame? The problem with the scientific nature of things is that it leaves out that which we can not quantify.

Once, in a past life of mine, the conditions were not right to set anything ablaze. A pile of old newspapers, in an old home, sat for years, unread and left alone. The stories, the words, the ink, the paper, they all generate their own heat. Tales needing to be told and felt and moved another way; the written word not enough for the energy they contained. Trees that had been cut, washed, bleached, refined, beaten down into thin sheets of paper, needing to be born again. Ink starving to get back to being a plant, putting its roots down in the soil, participating in the essential act of the earth breathing.

And so the paper and the stories and ink all sat and sat, their heat building up within them, getting hotter and stronger until one day, it could not take it any longer, and the whole thing burst into flame.

A fire is an event or occurrence, but it also is very much a whole thing, all its own.

24
Amy

"Why is this so hard to chew?" I ask, my mouth full of chocolate that stubbornly sticks to a drop of saliva, drying it up like rain that falls in the sand.

"Do you have any water?" I want to grab the bowl of water on the altar, but I have a feeling that is not what it's precisely for. Dr. Lauren gets up quickly, her startled eyes giving her away. *This is not supposed to happen, is it?* Grabbing the pitcher on the counter, she brings it over to me quickly, the water spilling on the way because of her rushed steps. I chug straight out of the spout. But no matter how much water I drink, I barely can get the chocolate to break up in my mouth; chewing what now feels like gum or a piece of tar, I take the hard chunk of chocolate out of my mouth and bite off pieces, chugging water in between.

"This is *good*," I say, giving Dr. Lauren a thumbs up. "Very...exotic." *Just wash it down; it's like swallowing a pill.* Water spills all over my face, dribbles down my chin, and I gasp for air, all while trying to be calm, cool, and collected. Like a deer caught in headlights, Dr. Lauren stares at me, horrified by the scene unfolding before her. *She knows I didn't choose the right one. This is all because the actual mushroom was heavier.*

Once I've forced every last bit down my throat, I drink the remaining water in the pitcher, desperately trying to wet the dry dust the chocolate has left behind. I gulp, making the loudest swallowing sounds I have ever heard, and when the ordeal is over, I am aware of how utterly horrified Dr. Lauren seems to be.

"Ok, I am ready." I take a deep breath and try to look as Zen as possible. It takes her a beat to regain her composure. Clearing her throat, she pretends what just happened was normal. "Wow, okay. Are you okay?" Her shock has turned to concern, and if I didn't know any better, I'd say she looks almost anxious. *Aren't I the one with anxiety?*

"Yeah, I think so. It was just..*dry*." A cough escapes my mouth, and I try and swallow the lump I fear may be there forever.

"Tell me about your experience weighing the mushroom and the chocolate." Dr. Lauren shifts her weight so she can comfortably sit on one of the pillows.

Oh shit. She knows. I should have known I couldn't lie to her and get away with it.

"Well," I begin. A quick look in her eyes makes me retreat to staring at my hands. *She is here to serve you, not punish you. Maybe this is part of my process.* "The mushroom weighed more," I mumbled inaudibly.

"What? I can't hear you," she leans in closer to me, and now it is evident by the rapid rising and falling of her breath that she, too, is anxious. Knowing this triggers the same response in me. Moments ago, I feared being caught lying, but now, I fear much worse. Despite my husband's warnings, I had googled "bad mushroom trips" the night before I came to her house. In hindsight, that was a foolish idea.

Most stories of "bad trips" sounded more like my daily routine. People have reported experiencing fear, grief, insanity, isolation, physical distress, and paranoia. *This sounds like a Monday afternoon before the wine kicks in.* However, on rare occasions, the mushrooms can be poisoned or "laced" with other drugs. I realize, at this moment, that I never actually checked Dr. Lauren's credentials, where she sourced her mushrooms from, or looked at that damn packet that I am sure had a list of contradictions. *Fuck me.*

"The mushroom weighed more," I say louder, articulating my words this time.

"I see." Dr Lauren says, her lips pursed like Meryl Streep's when James Holt showed her his new collection. *Catastrophe.*

25
Dr. Lauren

At least she answered honestly, helping me narrow down what could have gone wrong. She chewed and swallowed that piece of chocolate like a cow and it's cud. Even in my years of practicing, I never have seen the body outright reject a substance. Sure, it is common for people to vomit shortly after taking the psychedelic, but this is actually a sign it's integrating. The body's way of getting rid of anything extra so the medicine can absorb into the gut as fast and as potent as possible. Whatever happens in the gut occurs in the brain. But from the looks of it, the medicine didn't even want to make it down to the gut. I think *I should have listened to Tom* for the tenth time this morning.

"Well, there is much to discuss here as to why you went against what you knew your body wanted, but I am inclined to see if some of this reveals itself when the medicine kicks in." My voice is stern, like a teacher disappointed in her student. I am like a duck on the water, calm on the surface but paddling like hell underneath. My heart rate is increasing with each stare she is giving me. She is awaiting my expertise to tell her what to do next and reassure her that she will be okay and that this is normal. *This is not normal; this is a catastrophe.*

I contemplate texting Tom, but I don't want to be unprofessional. If I excuse myself, she will know I am panicking, and if I pull out my phone in front of her, she will know I lied about the house being a dead zone. It really only is in one corner of the room. In a split-second decision, mostly to buy me some time, I decide to proceed as normal.

"Let's have you lie down and take long, deep breaths as we wait for the mushrooms to work." Getting up, I smooth out the blanket and adjust the pillows so she can rest her head.

"How long will it take to kick in?" She begins to move; the rustling of the sequins is the only sound breaking the palpable silence.

"About twenty minutes." I pat the pillow, motioning her to lie down. Grabbing the weighted blanket, I place it over her to calm her body. *I wish I had another for me.*

"Let's practice one deep inhale and exhale together. Breathe in…breathe out….breathe in….breathe out." I am coaching her and myself at the same time.

"Good, Amy. That's right. Your breath reminds you that you are safe." *Safe? Maybe.* I begin to sweat, my hands clammy, and my breath is not working. *Just give her the spiel.*

Attempting to keep a steady breath and calm, soothing voice, I say the speech I've said a million times. "In a few minutes, the mushrooms will begin to kick in. You will notice a shift in perception and mood. As time passes, it will increase until you reach the Peak of the experience. This is where you will experience hallucinations, a distorted sense of time, and a fertile ground for introspection. You will still be able to hear me and talk to me. Once this phase ends, you will reach a plateau in your trip. You will still be able to feel the effects of the psilocybin, but your mind will be more alert. Here, we will begin unpacking what happened during the peak. I will write down everything you say, so don't worry about holding on to any thoughts. That which needs to stay with you will, and that which needs to be let go will disappear after your trip. This stage can last a few hours, but you will have no sense of time. I will be with you each moment; you can talk as much, or as little, as you want."

Her eyes are closed, and she is breathing deeply, her face seeming calmer than it was. Mine, on the other hand, does not. *I must get a hold of Tom.*

"I am going to put on some sound bowl music to help ease you in your transition. I am also going to the kitchen to gather more water and then the closet for a few more blankets, should we need them. You lie here, relaxing your body, until I return." I pat her arm gently, and only when she nods in understanding do I get up and head straight for my phone.

Ducking into the bathroom, I quietly shut the door and dial Tom's number. I climb into the bathtub, lying down with a towel over my head, hoping it serves as a sound barrier. *Ring. Ring. Ring.* No answer. It goes to voicemail. I try again. Same thing. *What the hell could he possibly be doing? He doesn't have a real job.* I try again. And again. Until I have called ten times, I know my time is up. She will wonder why I'm not making any noise or haven't returned like I said I would. Hopping out of the tub, I flush the toilet for good measure. Flipping on the water in the sink, I quickly rattle a text message to Tom.

"Hi. Thank you again for delivering the chocolate. I'm sorry, I can't remember what you said, but what type of mushrooms are in the chocolate? What are the other ingredients?" Sent.

The music is still playing, and I see Amy resting soundly on the pillows. It's been about 7 minutes since she forced down the chocolate. "You're doing great." I say as calmly as I can. I flutter around the house as quietly and quickly as possible, my clothes bustling at my ankles. Grabbing a few blankets from the closet, I check my phone to see if Tom has answered. Nothing yet. I shoot off another text: "Hello? I am in a bit of a situation here. Where are you?" I know I am sounding more frantic and borderline rude, which I can't afford after how I acted at his house. But I don't know what else to do. I send a police car light emoji.

I walk back into the room, the pile of blankets so high I can not see what is in front of me, and I stub my toe on the edge of the altar. The flame flitters in annoyance, the candle rocking back and forth. "Oh shit!" I say aloud, dropping the pile of blankets to grab the candle. The blankets, unfortunately, land directly on Amy's unexpecting face.

"What the fuck?" A muffled but startled yell comes from Amy. *Phew. That was close,* I think, as I steady the candle upright—another jolt to the nervous system.

"I'm so sorry!" I gasp, removing the blankets from her. *Welcome to amateur hour.*

She smirks at me, confused, annoyed, and dare I say; she brings out her resting bitch face. *I deserve it.* I gently smile back, tip-toeing around her to head to the kitchen. People on trips don't generally eat or drink. But she doesn't know this, and I need something to keep my hands busy. Pulling out a tray, I grab anything that could pass as a snack: a few string cheeses, the bottom of the box of crackers, a few mandarins left in the fruit bowl, and a handful of Jolly Ranchers.

"How are you doing, Amy? Have you noticed any changes yet?" I ask as I refill the water pitcher.

"Nope, not yet. How long has it been?" She inquires, her voice sounding like she knows she's being bought and sold.

I check my phone. Tom still hasn't answered, and his read receipts have not been turned on. I send another litany of messages, this time each as a separate one, in hopes that the constant ringing or vibrating gets his attention:

Tom, I need help!

My client could barely swallow the chocolate.

We are about 15 minutes post-consumption, and there are no signs of an altered state.

HELLLLLLLP.

B. COIL

26
Jane

As soon as I knock, I immediately regret it. *What am I thinking? Getting an almost stranger who is high on mushrooms to vouch for me is not the ideal scenario.* For a brief moment, I see myself: a delusional and maybe-knocked-up young woman who does not believe the imaging or expert opinion of her doctor but is relying on a practical stranger to confirm that I am, in fact, pregnant. But it's too late. I hear footsteps approaching. *I think there's still time to run;* looking down the stairs, I (breathlessly) climbed to get to the door. *I could hide in the pine trees, but she'd see my bike which isn't precisely a getaway vehicle.* The hill was tough, but I figured going down would be easy, and you can't beat the views. After the doctor's appointment, I drove home and put my bike in my car. Leaving the car at the grocery store gave me an alibi if someone were to ask later. I wasn't committing a crime going to Dr. Lauren's house, but I did fear what I might find here.

I had heard some rumors about her around town, but I didn't tell Amy that. The consensus was that Dr. Lauren was a bit of a wild card. I hadn't spoken to a local who had attended one of her retreats, but there have been many "before and after" portraits of the men going through there. The grocery store is such a central hub for gossip, word of the standoffish yet polished and polite men that grab a few snacks, a pack of gum, and a magazine and then Ubers up to her house and comes down a few days later looking disheveled, crying on the phone with his wife, spreads fast. Usually, an apology comes out of his mouth, and promises are made until he gets a smoothie to eat and then an Uber to the nearest airport. No one knows what really happens here, but it doesn't seem *insignificant*. *It's good I'm here early*, I convince myself, trying to feel less manic about my situation and instead, placing the need on Amy. *She might be in real, actual trouble.*

But now, seeing the run-down A-frame house, I realize that even if Amy needs rescuing, it's not like I can get her *and me* down the hill in record time *on my bike*. Especially since Dr. Lauren could easily hop in her Volvo, parked in the dirt outside her house, and run us off the road. *I should come back tomorrow, as planned, with my car.* I begin to turn, about to break for it when the door swings open behind me.

"Hi. Can I help you?" I turn at the sound of her voice. *Dr. Lauren*, I assume. She is not what I thought she would be. I imagined sporadic and messy, noisy eyes that were distant and unclear, something more like the witch in Hansel and Gretel, ready to devour whoever stepped foot in her home. But she is the opposite. She has warm, kind eyes with wild curls that fall elegantly into place. Her face, covered in scars, is like a mosaic, and it intrigues me instead of frightens me because of her big smile and even bigger eyes. There is an innocence that I didn't expect. *I am right where she wants me.*

"I'm looking for Amy?" I pose it as a question instead of an answer to what I'm doing here. Her face shows her surprise, her eyes widen, and she looks behind her. I peer behind her to see if I can see what she does, and sure enough, in the back room, I make out a silhouette of a woman who might be Amy.

Lying on the floor, surrounded by pillows. *Oh shit.* I didn't calculate that she may already be on her mushroom trip.

"I'm so sorry; I needed to talk to her but didn't realize she may already be…tripping or whatever. I can come back." I back down the stairs, wishing I could disappear and fade into the background. But before I reach the bottom step, Amy appears at the door, a huge smile spreads across her face when she sees it's me.

"Jane!" she squeals, like we were best friends in high school, and I've arrived at the sleepover. I walk back up the steps and am bombarded by her hug, which almost knocks me over.

"What are you doing here?" she asks, grabbing my shoulders and searching my face for answers. Her look of surprise turns to concern when I don't respond immediately. Looking me right in the eye, getting close, she inquires again, this time more pointedly, "Are you okay? Is something wrong with the baby?"

I can't handle her kindness and am overcome with fear for my baby's embarrassment. I came here and interrupted her session only to ignite the grief I feel all over again when she feels so much like a *mother.* I try to tell her what is going on, but the tears beat me to it; I sob, head in my hands on the dusty steps of a stranger's house.

"It's ok, I am here. I am here," she cradles my head in the crook of her neck and lets me cry, stroking the hair on the back of my head. *This is what it feels like.* I can't help but think. I never had a mother in my teen or adult life, and everything in this moment tells me I missed more than I thought I had.

"Let's go inside and see if we can get to the bottom of this." Taking my hand, Amy leads me up the stairs, passing Dr. Lauren, who looks disconcerted—and I can't say that I blame her. Amy mouths, "I'm sorry" to her as we pass but doesn't wait to see Dr. Lauren's reaction. I hear the door shut behind us.

As my eyes adjust to the light, I am taken aback at the beauty of the inside of the house. I take it all in full of velvet in what can only be described as royal colors. Pillows of every color, the great pine trees letting select rays of light in, some landing on an altar. I see the mushroom and am immediately reminded of what I have interrupted.

"Have you already eaten the mushroom? I should have waited and come when you asked, but I needed to see you immediately." I wait for an answer that frees me from my guilt.

"Why don't we all sit down, and you can catch me up on precisely what is happening here? I'm Dr. Lauren." Stretching out her hand to me, I shake it instinctively, "I'm Jane. Thank you for letting me in. I am so sorry, I just-"

"Let's take a breath, ok? I'll get you some water, and we can start from the beginning." She turns on her heel, her loose clothes flowing behind her, leaving a scent of lavender and vanilla behind her.

Amy is already sitting on one of the round cushions and pats a teal one beside her for me to sit. "Can I use the bathroom?" I whisper to Amy, afraid Dr. Lauren woun't allow me the courtesy.

"Of course!" Amy's cheerful response bellows in the quiet home, and Dr. Lauren looks at me from the kitchen and smiles.

"It's right down the hall on your left," she says.

The bathroom is bigger than I expected, given the house's look on the outside. Its tile seems to have been redone recently, and the hand towels are fluffy and look like they just came out of the box. Everything on the outside of the house is a deterrent to visitors, but the inside is welcoming, bright, charming, and, dare I say, boho chic. *What a strange combination.* I bide my time.

Whatever happens next, it must be precise and calculated.

Sitting next to Amy feels like home. Her hands rest on my knees when I settle into criss-cross applesauce as my chosen position.

"She's great, you're in good hands." Amy comforts me, squeezing my knee before placing her hands back in her lap.

I want to yell everything out before Dr. Lauren returns. Certainly, a diagnosis exists for someone who doesn't believe their doctor. I play out a scene in my mind in which I tell them about the events that led me to their front door. The positive pregnancy test, the morning sickness, the ultrasound results, the negative urine test, and, of course, the doctor's concerned look as I ran out of the room. I picture them listening intently until the last bit. Dr. Lauren's face turns from empathetic listening to deranged concern, her Rolodex of diagnoses landing on the one she sees fit. She slowly takes Amy's hand and draws her back behind her, standing and protecting Amy from me, taking away the closest thing I have felt to having a mother since mine died. I hear conflicting voices in my head. One of them says she *would only be doing her job*, rolling her eyes in disgust at my disguised altruism. But the other seems more reasonable: *You can't let that happen. You've lost your mother once; you can't risk it again.*

"Jane!" her voice interrupts my thoughts. She is standing above me, holding a glass of water. Amy laughs nervously.

"Sorry, I was daydreaming," I say, feeling sick. *This was a huge mistake. You can not tell her the whole truth.* Another, more rational voice tells me calmly: *You can trust me*, she whispers somewhere deep in my gut.

Dr. Lauren completes the triangle by sitting atop a magnetic pillow and begins her inquiry, "So, how do you two know each other?" I let Amy speak first.

Amy's version of our meeting fascinates me. The order of events is how I would have placed them, but the way she sees me is overly generous, using words like "intelligent," "beautiful," and "wonderful company." She leaves out the vomiting in the bathroom, the ghost of my dead mother that lurks in all my tears, and the one-night stand that put my dad and me at odds. *This is what it means to have someone in my corner;* I think as I smile in gratitude at her, my cheeks pink with pride.

Dr. Lauren listens intently, nodding in all the right places, her approval shown in smiles and a genuine interest in the story unfolding. But still, the elephant in the room lingers: *What the hell is she doing here?* I can sense the question, so I beat her to the next round of inquiries, yelling, "Why aren't you already tripping?"

It's a clumsy and defensive question that appears more like I am pointing fingers than interested. Exchanging nervous glances between them, Amy speaks first.

"Well, I did, but it didn't work." She looks at Dr. Lauren, then down at her hands. *Is she embarrassed?* I can't tell. I look pointedly at Dr. Lauren to fill in the gaps.

"I'm afraid we've had an issue with the psychedelics that Amy ingested. I've never had this happen, but it's possible that they don't have the effect we hope for sometimes. Or, in this case, no effect at all."

I am so happy I am not the only one who is being questioned in no specific terms for making things up. I can't help but smirk. I always do this in awkward moments. One time, I was at the store, and a vast celebrity died; I can't even remember which one, but one of my coworkers was crying hysterically as *if she knew him.* And I just burst out laughing. The more I tried to compose myself, the more intense my laugh became. My boss had to escort me to the breakroom, and I was instructed to stay until I could have a straight and empathetic face. It took me three attempts and 20 minutes.

"Is there something funny to you?" Dr. Lauren asks, more than a little agitated. *Uh oh, here comes the giggles.* But then I see Amy, and her face is red, not because she's suppressing laughter. Her body is hunched over, her knees curled up to her face, her chin resting on them. Her refusal of eye contact with me or Dr. Lauren softens my desire to point the finger at someone else besides me. *Does she think this is her fault?* I wonder, wishing Dr. Lauren wasn't in the room.

"No, I'm sorry." I mumble, embarrassed at my inability to read the room. The nuance of the situation is wholly lost on me, and my youth is glaringly apparent. Two grown women, both wiser than me by at least a million experiences, and my blinders are on so tightly I only respond out of high school petulance. I notice a small inhale in Amy, followed by a stuttered exhale, and I die a tiny death in front of them both. An all-too-familiar thought runs through my mind: *I never have deserved a mother.*

And I believe it to be true. I have never deserved a mother, and maybe I don't deserve to be a mother either. All the evidence I've gathered in favor of my chance to rewrite the story, to have a connection with a daughter that will somehow redo the prophecy that has hung over my whole life, maybe it's karma, a trick from the universe of a sealed fate. Maybe my greatest fear has always been right: I will be alone forever.

"It's not her fault; It's mine," Amy says sheepishly. Dr. Lauren shifts uncomfortably. *There is something she isn't saying.* I know it's not my business, but I feel defensive of Amy. "How do you know that?" I retort, doing my best to sound innocent and curious. My eyes stay locked on Amy.

"She gave me specific instructions, and I didn't follow them," Amy says, clearing her throat halfway through as if she's trying to swallow this pill.

"Is this true?" I look at Dr. Lauren. The warmth I felt from her when she opened the door has gone out the window. I don't trust her. She has guilt written all over her face. I may not deserve a mother, but Amy deserves the truth.

"I did give her instructions, but—" she begins. I can't help myself. The heat inside me is building, and I am angry with her for ruining Amy's chance at getting what she came here for. I feel irrationally protective of her, thinking of the baby inside me and what it would be like if it's true, if she's actually there, and one day I get to protect her. *Is this a test?* I'll take it.

"But what?" I ask, not letting her finish her sentence.

"Please calm down, Jane. It's really okay. I'm sure I can just take another dose, and we will start the process over." Amy is comforting me now, which makes me more enraged. The second dose must be the mushroom sitting in the cup on the altar, along with the feather, bowl of water, and candle whose flame is standing eerily still. I get up, grab the mushroom, and hand it to Amy.

"Here, take it. As soon as it kicks in, I'll leave." Amy hesitantly takes it from me, looking to Dr. Lauren for approval.

"I'm afraid you can't do that, Amy. Even if the first dose didn't work, it still is in your system, and if you take another, you could overdose." Dr. Lauren sounds remorseful, but I imagine she's practiced these lines a million times over again.

"You are a LIAR!" I scream, startling Amy and Lauren but igniting something inside me. Looking at Dr. Lauren, I feel the rage of everyone who has been just like her in my life come to the surface. The longer I stare at her eyes and disfigured face, the longer she becomes a stand-in for all the doctors who have done me wrong: the one today who denied me of my baby, the one who put me on my meds when I was younger instead of listening to me, upping my dose every time I had an "episode," and the ones who couldn't save my mom. I don't see her face anymore; I know the face of all the doctors who have entirely fucked me over. And I will not let her do the same to Amy.

The thing about rage is that it starts somewhere deep inside you, like a little flame deep in your belly, and if left alone, it will soon dwindle or die out. But when fueled by memories and faces from the past, by all the pain that goes with it, the fire spreads from your gut to your throat, making space for the roar you never got to shout, and then it ignites in your limbs; your arms and legs moving rapidly as if they are on fire too. The energy built up inside you is too much, and you have to move it to get it out. I get up and pick up the bowl of water on the altar, chucking it at the ground, screaming everything I wish I had said to all the doctors before her. "Fuck you!" and it feels so good to let some of the fire out that I let it take over. I grab the next object I can throw, a small crystal she has on the coffee table, and I chuck it at the window, missing it due to my horrible aim. The sheer excitement of the sound and release that would have caused it had I hit it spurred me on for more. I stomp around the room, thrashing my arms until my hand latches on to something I can throw, and I land on handmade coasters. Flinging them like frisbees, I throw them all around the room, not caring what they hit. I am just happy to release the monster fire that has been inside of me almost my entire life. "I hate you!" I shout with the first disc, it flying towards the front room, bouncing off the couch and onto the floor. "I won't take your stupid pills!" I scream again, hurling the next coaster toward the kitchen. "It is *my baby!*" I yell, the coaster hitting the glass panel on the microwave, causing a crack that comes with a beautiful, startling sound. I am out of coasters, but I continue to thrash around the room, grabbing everything I can and throwing it to the ground and against the wall, shattering the glass items fueling my next throw. "This is for all the doctors exactly like you," I yell as the vase in her kitchen hits the floor, water flowers and glass spreading across the room.

"Jane! Jane, stop!" I hear Amy screaming, standing up, and reaching out to me, but she can't help me now. She can't mother me now; I am beyond mothering. I look her in the eyes, a brief moment of reprieve from the rage. While still holding her gaze, I kick the entire altar to the ground, "It isn't fair!" I think of everyone who worshiped a god that rejected me and my dad and my dead mother out of their heavenly gates.

Amy is pleading with me to stop, but I won't. I can't. It feels too good to let loose everything that has stacked inside me. Finally, a match is lit and ready to burn it all down. All the years of grief, anger, embarrassment, and decades of unanswered questions finally get to burn and turn to blackness, the same color of the ache I have made a home with. I look around the room for something else to throw and see Dr. Lauren holding the candle from the altar in the corner. She must have grabbed it before I kicked the altar to the ground. *Why is she protecting it?*

I zero in on her, one hand gripping the candle, the other cupping the flame like a birthday candle delivered to the birthday girl. *Happy fucking birthday to YOU.* Approaching her slowly, I want to destroy the candle, the flame, and anything else she finds important. She didn't stop me from breaking everything in this room, but she is guarding this candle with her life.

"Give me the candle, Dr. Lauren," I tell her, a warning in my tone. I don't know what I am going to do with it. Blowing it out seems like a very anticlimactic ending to the rage-fest I just engaged in.

"Jane," she says, her voice quivering, "I am sure we can talk about whatever bothers you. But please, please don't take the candle. It's the only thing I have left."

"Don't therapize me! Why should *you* have something you care about? I don't have anyone or anything! My dad hates me, my mom died, I have no friends, a boy fucked me and left me and a baby that is no longer growing inside me." I seethe, stepping closer to Dr. Lauren.

"Oh, Jane, I'm so sorry," Amy says from behind me. I ignore the softness of her voice. She continues, "Is that why you came? Did you just find out?"

I keep my eyes on Dr. Lauren. My silence will answer for itself.

"I lost a baby too, Jane." Dr. Lauren confesses as she backs herself further into the corner. "I can help you, I can." She is pleading with me, begging. I look at the fear in her eyes, and I almost take the bait. I almost forgive her and everything she represents. I nearly ignore the fire still burning in me and let the comfort and solution she is promising to put out the flame. But then, I notice something I hadn't until now. With her arms intent on protecting the candle, her sleeves have stopped clinging to her wrists, and her bare skin reveals a tattoo on her arm: a wild California poppy.

A deep pain sears through me; I grip my abdomen tightly, and I swarm. I feel her squirm from the inside of my womb space. She is one with the fire inside me, squirming and dancing, and I know I can not stop now. I grab a the tube of oil paint and a brush that sits out, nonchalantly by a blank canvas in the living room. Instinctually, I graffiti a bright red heart with my initials and Poppy's on the tree trunk that sits strong and bare in the middle of the living room. My whole life has been a black hole of loneliness; no one understood what it was like to be me. For the first time, this rage, this fire inside, feels exactly right. Since my mother died, every cell in my body has been on fire, but everyone around me has tried to put it out. The diagnosis, the pills, the doctor visits, the therapists; no one has ever allowed me just to let it burn.

I need Amy and Dr. Lauren to witness what it's like to be me. I need my outside world to mirror my inside world. Then, I will finally not be alone. I look to Amy, who stands, fearful and concerned, next to me. I know what I need to do. "I'm sorry," I say to her, and I grab the candle out of Dr. Lauren's hand in a split second. With one swift throw, I chuck the candle at the tree. The universe is on my side, the candle flips through the air, and everything is in slow motion, time standing still. The flame somehow escapes the oxygen that threatens to put it out until it comes in contact with the fresh oil paint on the tree trunk, and I watch as the whole tree ignites, starting with the burning heart I graffitied only moments before. There we were, her and I, finally burning the whole fucking thing down.

27
Fire

I feel the wind hit me as she pulls me towards her—the fury of her breath, a duel of opposing forces. The air moving through me forces me to work harder to keep my heat alive, *and* the air brings more oxygen, which gives me the runway I need to burn faster and more robustly. She throws me, and I whip through the air; the only thing saving me is my own will to live. I extend my heart, searching for more explosive things as I topple over and over and over and over again. Nothing catches me until, just before the base of the candle hits the tree, my heat extends and finds its match. Whatever she used, it was meant for me to find. She knew I was more than a tiny flame, coddled by a woman who used me to hide her pain.

I explode, following the shape she has made in the tree. A heart. It will take me less than 30 seconds to spread, the smoke already filling the room by then. This is my chance. I want to see what I am made of and feel the fury of my ancestors, who the gods worshiped and adored. I have been tamed for decades and have been set free.

As I engulf the trunk of the tree and climb my way up to the roof, I hear screams around me, but I keep burning and spreading and engulfing. With rage and freedom, I penetrate the roof, and suddenly, I am flowing like water down the sides of the house, and the whole thing is inside my womb. I will give birth to something new where my captivity once was.

28
Peggy

She is in the coming down, the other side of the trip that I can only use one word to describe: sweet serenity. Depending on how it went, the front end of the journey can be an explosion of things, disorientating. We have multiple playlists to use that Jake has curated, so I trust the cadence. On the descent, a favorite from Trevor Hall plays, *The Lime Tree,* and I can't help but sing along. I am no singer, unlike my sister, but I make up for what I lack in tune and sincerity.

Spark a match and watch the candle burn
The wick runs out and then love takes its turn
On fallen angels and broken sounds
We will last past the final round
It took a while for you to find me
But I was hiding in the lime tree
Above the city in the rain cloud
I poked a hole and watched it drain out (ayy, ayy)

I learned in my first 100 patients that I did alongside Tom that I have to bring myself into the equation. There is an element of mystery that I must latch on to, not giving it any more religious meaning than is already swirling in my over-thinking mind. I am exactly where I need to be. London is exactly where she needs to be. Some elements, some universal pull, have put us together, and just as she needs to show up as her full self, I do, too. So I sing. I sing loudly, letting the music take over, as I ride the wave of the sweet descent, too.

One of the greatest joys of being a Guide is that even when I can not see what my patients see or hear what they hear, I am on the Journey with them. Maybe it's the placebo effect or the playlist, but when they Journey, we do, too. So I sit, singing, and watch her face soften, enjoying the coming down.

It took a while for you to find me
But I was hiding in the lime tree
Above the city in the rain cloud
I poked a hole and watched it drain out, yeah
It took awhile for you to find me
But I was hiding in the lime tree
Above the city in the rain cloud
I poked a hole and watched it drain out, yeah

I feel the weight of the journey begin to ease its way out of my shoulders, down first my arms and then my legs until I am lying down next to London, enjoying the unspoken solace I feel with her presence next to me. I gave her what I could during our session, but I often wonder if it was enough. She repeatedly yelled, "Help me, Peggy! Help!" I answered her as I knew how: "I'm right here, London. You aren't alone." Inside, however, I struggled. My mind raced through its manuals of tools and tricks I've learned along the way. Her body twisted and turned, convulsed at times. She yelled, screamed, and cried, a torturous experience to watch and not be able to help. I held her with energy and space, wanting to do more and fix it for her, knowing

I could not. I saw before she told me that this was not an easy trip. I wanted it to be good, calming, beautiful, and serene for her. But I learned long ago that we can not impose anything on medicine; it does exactly what it needs to do.

And so we trust it. If we can't trust it, then what else do we have? I look to my left and see her calm and steady breath again. I am grateful we have arrived back here. And I wait. I wait for her to move, to see life in her fingertips or the fluttering of her eyes. I hum.

Finally, she rolls out her wrists. Her eyes open, adjusting to life again. She sees me. She has landed back.

"Hi," she says, sitting up slowly, cross-legged. Her face is different now. I sit, knee to knee, something I do at the Sangha with my teacher.

"Have some water." I hand her a glass. She takes a sip, then furiously drinks down the rest, immediately refilling her cup and drinking it again. Again, I wait. We must now integrate, and as protocol calls for, I hand her an iPad, the blue light blaring into her eyes, causing her to squint. She must fill out a questionnaire that PCMI has put together that asks many questions, asking her to put into words what's occurred beyond words.

She stares at the device. She turns it off and puts it to her side.

"Not yet. Not now." She looks me straight in the eye, the anxious and meek girl who began the journey now a figure in the review mirror.

"After you fill it out, we can continue talking, but that survey is necessary." I pick up the iPad and hand it back to her. She takes it from my hand and places it on the couch behind her.

"No." She is not mad; she is not being defiant, I realize. *She has a boundary.*

My job is to journey, to guide, and to keep the client safe from start to finish, so I don't push it.

"Ok," I tell her, nodding in agreement. She is still safe here.

"Where do you want to start?" I ask her, not prepared for the integration to begin. I don't have my legal pad, recorder, or anything else I usually have. It's just me and her, and it's an unusual experience for the perpetual rule follower in me. *This is an intuitive art.* I remind myself.

She takes a deep breath, closes her eyes, and begins to tell me what her journey was like.

29

London

"Awake" isn't quite the right word for it, but I wasn't asleep either. I stood. I was. I am.

I didn't realize the storehouse of memories my brain has held; in the journey, it would bring them up in a narrative I could make sense of. My earlier bouts with therapy involved the dredging up of past wounds, the wonderings and "what ifs" of the paths I didn't take. I always thought therapy was painful. But this, there was one path, no little trails that showed me what could have been, only cairns of love stacked on the way. The road was winding and beautiful, a masterwork of art of vibrant colors and hues that were dynamic and moving. My whole life was moving; it was *alive*.

The dissolution of right and wrong came first. I saw my life in front of me, in all its moon phases, and it was *correct*. There was no possible other way it could have unfolded. As soon as I knew that, *I* dissolved next.

Like a balloon popping and revealing a million pieces of confetti flying into the landscape, some paving the road and others finding their paint-by-number square in scenes from my life. I became one with the journey, my choices, and the traumas. I was her; she was me, the ghost of my past and the one from my distant future.

Only a tiny piece of me remained, a little, small spark. The one that you find at the top of a candle, holding on, barely burning. Or, the leftover ember flitted away from the bonfire, desperate to hold on to life. As I know myself to be, a small part stayed glowing.

I met all the ghosts from my past, present, and hopeful future. I saw the shadow and light sides of me, the grand playwright in my head, and the scenes it had written. I watched it all play out, these parts of me that were parts all their own. I witnessed the fierce love and protection they had for me, the lengths they went to protect me: when I was five and in that bedroom when I was ten and left without a house, when I was twenty and couldn't save him, and every futile liferaft I threw myself in between it all.

I am coming down, and I can hear Peggy singing. Her voice is soothing and calm, a welcomed bridge to coming back to consciousness. She never left me, holding space for this sacred journey.

"Hi," I say, sitting up slowly, cross-legged. Peggy's gaze is quiet yet expectant. She has an eagerness about her, waiting to see what I will say, but as if she could wait all day. She repositions herself close to me so that our knees are touching. My first human contact with the real world.

"Have some water." She hands me a glass. I take a small sip at first, and then my mouth can't get enough. I drink the whole cup down easily and ask for more. I am not ready to talk just yet. She waits.

Suddenly, her presence shifts a tiny bit, but I am more aware now. She is thinking about something else, a "to-do" with impending blank boxes she must check off. She hands me an iPad, the bright blue, artificial light serves as a reminder of reality. It threatens to reduce my experience down into categories of "somewhat agree" and "totally disagree."

I stare at the device, my whole body rejects it. *How can I put my psyche into a box?* Taking it from her, I turn it off and put it to my side. The room is dark again, except for the tiny spark that I can feel inside of me still glowing.

"Not yet. Not now." I look at her straight in the eye, telling her what I need and for the first time in my life feeling clear about what that is. I feel the spark, just below my navel, increase in courage.

"After you fill it out, we can continue talking, but that survey is necessary." She picks up the iPad and hands it back to me. Without thinking, I take it from my hand and place it on the couch behind me.

"No," I tell her. I am not mad; I know what I need; an odd but welcomed feeling. Peggy senses this shift in me, and honors it.

"Ok," she tells me, nodding in agreement. I am still safe here. The spark remains.

"Where do you want to start?" She asks, shifting in her seat. I take a deep breath, and begin.

30
Amy

"She was wild and afraid; she held everything that had ever happened to me." I begin slowly, trying to describe the indescribable. "But God, she was beautiful."

"Who was?" Peggy interjects, attempting to hide her excitement like a child waiting to open a present.

"Amy." That was her name. She was the first one that I met.

"Tell me about her," Peggy coaxes.

"She was anxious. On the verge of committing suicide, mentally unstable at times. She loved to mother those around her, maybe to a fault." I begin to choke up as I say these words, the barrier of meaning breaking through for the first time.

"Mothering." That is all Peggy responds. I wait. I let that word sink in, each letter falling into the deep places of my womb, like little letter magnets that do not spell the correct word on the refrigerator.

"She had two kids like me," I explain what I can remember about her. "Her life was just like mine, but all the things that I try to shove down and away, she was loud and honest about them."

"Tell me about your kids," Peggy replies.

A smile spreads; I couldn't stop it if I tried.

"My son, he's thirteen. He's full of life and joy, and he can make a game out of a cardboard box that would win a prize. My daughter, she's seven and the most creative and kind soul you'll ever meet."

"What is it like to mother them?" she asks, the magnet letters still in a pile at the bottom of her uterus.

"It's like lighting a candle." We both sit, contemplating the imagery that comes to mind. A birthday party. A vigil. A source of light when the power goes out. The expensive one that smelled so delicious it was worth every penny.

"How so?" Peggy asked, coming back from her own memories.

"They are the brightest lights I've ever known. When they came into this world, they brought me a sense of security and peace, as if I had a place in the world." I remember when I gave birth to them; both opened my heart in a way I had never imagined.

"They gave me a place to put my anxiety. I made my whole life about never letting the candle go out." I feel the familiar tightness of shame and real-life entering into my heart space. I try and breathe through it. I close my eyes and picture Amy again.

"It's ok. We have all the time in the world." Peggy sits forward, her knees pressing harder into mine, a reminder that I am not alone.

"Tell me more about Amy." Peggy brings her back to the foreground. There was something about Amy that felt familiar, like a homecoming of sorts. The details of the journey were so vivid, it was like I could reach out and touch it with my soul. Tactile, like an embroidery of love and vigilance disguised as attention to detail but the back all tangled up, knotted out of control. She was everything the teenage part of me was: giggly, petulant, lover of music and pop culture. I'd like to think I've outgrown such things, but I wonder if I grew up too fast; if this part of me had more to live. The underlying carefree spirit she embodied reminded me of things I used to love about myself.

"She was a wild, wonderful spirit, full of life and dreams, but piled on top was this crushing anxiety that buried all that glow underneath." Like being punched in the gut, my own words hit me in a place that threatens to disrupt everything inside of me. A wound buried so deep that uprooting it may cost me everything I have.

"What is she anxious about?"

I see Amy again, holding a large suitcase of emotions from everyone else but her: the burdens of being a teenager, the entanglement of fear and anxieties, the pressure of work, aging parents and family boundaries. She packed them all up in her suitcase, clothing herself with them all in the form of different patterns and textiles.

"She's afraid something might happen to her family. She loves them so much, it's like she's holding them all with a clenched fist, thinking she is protecting them."

"Who else is she protecting?" Peggy never breaks eye contact with me, even when I close my eyes. I can feel her gaze, a steadfast point of contact, a lighthouse in the stormy waters that I am in.

"Little London, when my house burned down."

"Tell me more." Peggy is the same way outside the journey as she was inside with me.

"I wasn't there; I came home to it. My whole life, in a pile of soot and ashes. Every picture, every stuffed animal, the walls around me, and the roof over my head." Eyes shut, I think back to that night, the lights from the firetrucks filling the night sky.

"How did that feel?" Peggy asks the same question that every therapist has asked me my whole adult life. I've never been able to put it into words: a total disconnection from the trauma. "Disassociation" is what they call it. But for the first time, I can finally feel it. Because when I look back on the scene, I am there, watching my house burn down in flames. The whole neighborhood is there, too, watching. Behind the yellow caution tape that I am privileged enough to be inside, my dad is talking to the firefighters, and my mother and sister are beside me. But so is Amy.

My eyes fly open at the realization. "She was there."

"Hold on to it, London. You are safe to go there." Peggy reassures me, her voice easing the tension in my chest.

"I think that was the night she was born. That Amy came alive inside of me. We watched the house burn, and I felt completely displaced, and that at any time, I could lose everything all over again." Tears begin to fall on my cheeks, a slow trickle of accepting the words that have always been inside but never spoken.

"Who is Amy, London?" Her question surprises me. I sit with it, allowing it to travel through my ears and into my mouth, down my throat, past my achy heart, and fall into the pit of my being, where the spark lives, the magnets still in disarray at the bottom of it.

Who is she?

I go back to my house burning down, and I try to find her again. I can't see her, but I can feel her. *Is she behind me?* I turn and look, but still no sign of her. I watch the house burn, the firemen's hoses barely making a dent. I feel a trembling in my hands, my whole body shaking, and suddenly, I do something I have never done before. I begin to unlace and relace my shoes. I furiously pull the string out of the holes as I sit on the hot pavement that only a Scottsdale summer can bring. I begin to put them back in, very precisely and meticulously, lacing them back up, one at a time, tying them at the top only to find that they are not exactly right, and so I start the whole process over again—the *beginning of my OCD.*

"She is the OCD part of me." The realization is earth-shattering. "I feel compassion for her, gratitude for her efforts to protect me. I feel sorrow and grief for little London, who needed Amy in such a desperate way. I picture myself, Amy, at the forefront every time I arranged my desk at least twenty times before falling asleep, or when later I didn't know why but couldn't start a project or go on a run unless it was the exact zero-hour. Amy, who took over as soon as the children were born, protected their light by covering it, hiding it, sanitizing, managing, protecting, and being aware that a flame without breath would most certainly die. And so Amy became the manager of the flames, taking mine away from me to keep theirs lit, a horrible cycle that has left us dimmed and me, extinguished completely."

"Amy is *you*. A beautiful, helpful part of you." Peggy says, understanding something that I barely do.

"I-I have lived my whole life arranging things ceremoniously to try and mitigate a tragedy. I've seen multiple therapists put on medicine, and no one has ever suggested my OCD to be beautiful, helpful, or remotely good. I've spent my life trying to banish, ignore, and cut it out." I stammer through the disconnection I feel as I say it.

"We aren't a mono-mind, London. We've been led to believe we are. But we are all made of multiple parts." Amy is right there again, almost like one of my limbs. "She is beautiful. Every part of her, mothering *someone*, mothering *you.* Full of life and ambition, but unable to get to it." I finish what Peggy has started; sharing details that feel sacred and important enough to give voice to.

"She wants to be a writer. She wants to tell a story that makes a difference. She wants to change the world and mother it into healing and wholeness. But she can't because her candle burned out."

"She has gone to great lengths to protect you, London. She is a *good* part that was forced into a *bad* role. Do you see the difference?"

I contemplate this reality. I think back to Amy, whom I met on my journey. There was an outside experience for Amy and an inner one, too. On the outside, she was vibrant and alive. She had it all together, a portrait of a perfect life. Her manicured nails, hair that never fell out of place, clothes, and make-up to the nines. Her children were fed every organic and grass-fed piece of food; their vitamins were always taken, the beds were made, and the house was vacuumed, a montage of suburbia. However, the gift the trip gave me was to have an inside experience with Amy, too. She is hollow. She has no light inside her, only a dark expanse that insists this is the only way.

"Can you access Amy now?" Peggy interrupts me at the perfect moment, and I stare straight into her hollow eyes.

"Yes, I am looking right at her," I answer, swallowing the lump in my throat.

"Ask her how old she thinks you are," Peggy suggests. I do. I wait.

"Twelve years old, going into seventh grade." Amy is confident of this.

"Tell her how old you are and see how she reacts."

"She is shocked. She had no idea."

"You're doing great." Peggy continues to ground the

moment, helping me stay present and know I am safe. She continues, "Ask her why she puts out your flame."

My flame. I ask her, and immediately she is defensive.

"She says a flame turns into a fire. She's not happy I am questioning her." I shrink back a bit, noticing my sudden desire to perform a ceremonious action on repeat to show her that I still think she has a place.

"Tell her you are thankful to her for keeping you safe. Tell her you know why she had to do it." Peggy doesn't seem afraid or intimidated by Amy at all. I try to match her tone as I approach Amy inside of me.

Whenever I was afraid, you gave me somewhere to put my energy. Thank you, Amy. Our little rituals made me feel safe and able to navigate the world. Without you, Amy, I would have crumbled.

"Ok, I did."

"How did she respond?"

"She seems proud. She knows she did her job well." I feel this deep in my bones. Amy has done her job so very well. My OCD, yes, has taken over at times, but mainly has kept me safe in this unsafe world. I have navigated every life change because Amy put my nervous energy somewhere, allowing me to ease enough to be social, to fall in love, and become a mother.

"Ask her if she didn't have to keep you safe. What other role would she like to do?"

"She says that if I were safe, she would help me dream again." My heart breaks a little at this realization. I can't remember the last time I dreamed or knew myself beyond my role as a mother and wife.

"Ask her if the dreams are the flame?"

"She says it is."

"Ask her why it would be bad for the flame to turn into a fire. Are all fires harmful, or can a prescribed burn be helpful?"

I sit with Peggy's question for an unknown amount of time. I try to continue the dialogue with Amy, but she yells at me to run and turn from this line of thinking. She reminds me that the burning down of the house is why she was forced into this role in the first place. She begs me not to listen, tells me stories of destruction, fears, and goes as far as to say that if my flame burns bright, I will end up burning it all down.

Burn it all down. Someone else is in the room inside my head. I don't have to tell Peggy this. She somehow already knows.

"Who else is there, London?" She inquires, her patience unparalleled. I remember the stop on my journey. Someone came to save Amy. Like a million puzzle pieces falling into place.

"Her name is Jane."

31
Peggy

A knock at the door jolts me out of our session. *Oh shit, they are here to collect the surveys.* I have lost the plot I usually follow and the protocol I teach to everyone I train. London is startled out of her inner work, turning to look at the door and then at me. I pause. *What should I do? Should I ignore it and move forward? Ask for an extension.* I am one of the Expert Guides, yet I am acting like an intern- all nervous and worried I will get into trouble. *You've made this program what it is. You can set the tone; you can change the tone. It's an intuitive art, remember?*

"London, can we take 5 for a minute? I need to speak with the team and tell them we need more time with the…survey." I don't want to pressure her, the glowing iPad hanging over her head, like I'm just interested in the data, not her humanity. Thankfully, she seems to understand.

"Can we continue after? I have to use the restroom anyway." I nod my head. Yes, even though I have no idea if we can continue with what we are doing. I point her toward the bathroom, and I slip out into the hallway as soon as she is inside. Jake, one of our trainees, is waiting outside. He is a lovely young man who wears a cowboy hat when he is not on official duty and has asked if cowboy boots count as "closed-toed shoes."

"Hi, Dr. Peggy. Do you have London's survey completed?" he asks, in his southern drawl.

"Um, not quite. I'm having an issue," I say, only a half-lie.

"Oh, with the iPad? I can grab you a new one." He turns his body toward the main office, but I grab his arm to stop him.

"No, with, um, the patient," I say, feeling bad. I'm blaming my driving off-course on London, but maybe I can use this as a unique case to bide more time.

"Oh really? I checked her in; she doesn't seem uncooperative." Jake looks at me earnestly, with worry in his eyes. He cares so much, and I know he will be one of our top Guides. The thought of him in my role one day makes me stiff. *Is that dread?* I can't pinpoint the feeling, especially because ethos is the work I love and was born to do. But something shifted in me today. I listened to London. She's not the first client I have worked with whose parts have come out. I am certified in the Internal Family System model and many other modalities. But her determination to integrate immediately, like she couldn't survive if we didn't, caught me off guard. She had a visible aversion to the iPad and the conceptualization of what can't be conceptualized. Even the explaining she is doing about Amy and meeting her on the path, I know, is a tiny droplet of what the experience was actually like.

"It's not that she is uncooperative; it's just more nuanced and complicated. I'm going to talk with Tom, so for now, just put in the notes that I don't have the data for you yet." He looks uncertain but pulls up London's file and flags it with the appropriate code.

I think their stories are codable as I make my way up to Tom's office.

Tom is the kindest supervisor I've ever had. We've been

friends for 30 years, starting this together back in the day. He's involved and hands-on, genuinely caring for the participants who come through our doors. In fact, he watched my interview with London and gave her the thumbs up despite my warning that she might be a more complicated case. I'm hoping that even though he's admitted thousands of patients, he remembers our conversation about this one.

I knock softly, not waiting for his reply before I enter. There could be a painting about the scene that I walk into. Tom is nothing if not consistent: a denim top and bottom, a big belt, and calloused hands that gave away his life before he was here. He's never admitted it, but it wouldn't surprise me if he grew his own mushrooms back in the day. He knows too much about the different types of psilocybin and how to administer them; he wrote the book on what we do here. No one does that if they haven't learned it by hands-on experience first. But I don't press him. It's part of his charisma.

"Ah, Peggy! The person I want to see." He gets up from his desk, shakes my hand, and then pulls me into a hug.

"Oh yeah?" I say, acting innocent. We take our seats on opposite sides of the desk.

"Yeah, a red flag just came through that you didn't turn in your data for your patient." He looks at me, both of us, knowing this is not only a breach of protocol but also the first time I've broken such protocol in three decades.

"Do you remember London? The complicated case you worked with me on during applications?" He nods, and I continue, "Well, I was right; she is proving to be more complicated than we thought. Her journey seemed intense, and she refused to answer the questionnaire." I pause and wait for it to sink in. I'm not sure what angle to use to play this. Indeed, she doesn't want to complete the protocol, but I know Tom will remind me that I am in charge. On the other hand, it's also true that something inside of me tells me forcing it on her will have a detrimental effect.

"She signed an agreement when she signed on to this. And in that agreement was that she would complete the survey in the appropriate amount of time. Legally, she's bound to this, Peggy." His tone is strong but soft. He reports to certain people who report to certain people who end up being a chain of our hands being tied.

"I know, but can we agree that the 'appropriate amount of time' isn't always the same for everyone?" I ask, knowing Tom has been in situations that require more nuance when he was a guide.

"How much time do you need? You're already an hour over what every other patient has been given." He is looking straight at me, and I know I have a little wiggle room.

"Can I get an overnight request?" I ask sheepishly, knowing this is out of the question. We only allow someone who has a medical reason to stay the night. And since she has no written physical medical conditions, I can't fudge that one.

"No, absolutely not. You know I can't do that, Peggy. What is this about?" Tom's looking directly inside me, the way only a person who has walked with you for half your life can do.

"Don't you ever feel like the way we end these sessions isn't enough? That words aren't the right modality?" I ask, thirty years of exasperation coming to the surface. I am upset at the man this medicine services. I want its magic to be fully realized to the very end.

"The human language isn't enough? Are you listening to yourself? The thing we have used to communicate for the entire history of humanity suddenly isn't enough for you?" I wince, my heart pounding. The old Tom never would have responded this way. At the beginning of this, Tom would have rolled his eyes at a survey, broken an iPad, and instead brought in plants and soil for patients to plant. But now, he's speaking a different language than I am. He sees what we are doing through the lens of data and investors, of only science and nothing of art.

"Tom, come on. Remember the old days? When we could do something more, something different? That allowed us to use our intuition. It's now watered down to this collection of data and numbers, of brain waves and measurable things that aren't measurable. If granted an overnight, I could bring in something, paints, music, dance, *anything other than the iPad*, for her to try to integrate better." I am pleading with him, my voice shaky, which I hate because I fear it denotes weakness. Women's passionate emotions are always mistaken for fragility.

"You want me to grant an unethical overnight so you can have craft time with your patient?" He is laughing at me, and it hurts.

"Tom, I am already breaking protocol. Her parts showed up, like a movie, and I began to sort through one with her, but another is on the way, and I don't know how many were on the scene. If she doesn't fully integrate, and we leave those parts disturbed and agitated, we risk a severe and negative psychiatric response." My voice is firm, a response to a feeling inside of me that I have not felt for a client in a long time. *Protective.*

He covers his ears, "Don't tell me about breaking protocol. You know I will have to report you, Peggy." He inhales deeply, his hands leaving his ears on the exhale. "Look," he continues, "I will give you three more hours, but that is it. That's all you get, and you can't run home and gather your little arts and crafts projects. Am I clear?"

"Yes," I say, standing up and shaking his hand profusely. "Thank you, thank you, Tom."

"Don't make me regret this, Peggy." He yells after me as I am already out his door, running down the isolated hall to the stairwell.

Three hours is not enough, but it gives me some time. I make it back to the room in record time, taking a deep breath to gather myself before I enter. It's been more than five minutes, but I don't think London will notice. I turn the handle, open the door, and there she is. Waiting for me, a soft smile on her face as I enter.

"Hi, sorry about the delay," I say to her. "Shall we continue?"

32
Jane

"Shall we continue?" She enters the room; seeing her sets my whole body ablaze again. The rage has yet to leave, and I place my hand on my belly as a reminder of why I did what I did.

"Tell me, London, about Jane." She smiles at me as she sits, her knees touching mine. The touch of her skin revolts me; how could she act like we are friends? We are opposing forces; I want revenge and to burn the whole thing down, and she wants to hide, keeping the flame small and barely able to breathe.

Without a word, I shift on my hips, moving backward so that we are no longer touching. She notices the adjustment and looks at me with curiosity.

"I apologize, London. We learn that touch can be a form of safe connection. Do you want your space at this moment?" *There's no fucking way she is accessing London,* I think, my resolve strengthening. I don't give her the satisfaction of an answer to her question; instead, as an attempt to be in charge, I begin to question her.

"Why is the flame so important to you?" I start with the last image in my mind, Dr. Lauren, in the corner, and instead of protecting Amy, she is fending for herself.

"I am not sure what you mean. Can you explain further?" Dr. Lauren feigns concern, wearing the same mask I saw her put on when Amy couldn't hold her own.

"*That* flame," I say, pointing to the candle on the table in the corner of the room. I am uncertain how it's still intact; I remember throwing it, exploding the tree, and the whole thing set on fire. When I woke up, I was here, in what I can only assume is a psychiatric ward of some kind, but the biggest question remains: *Why is she here, and why is she in charge?*

Dr. Lauren looks towards the candle, flickering softly in the corner of the room. She stares at it for too long, searching for another excuse or made-up lie that she will expect me to believe.

"How could you do that to her? She needed you; all you cared about was your candle!" I am up on my feet, my hands first at my sides, clenched, my nails digging into the palms of my hands. The pain of it feels good.

Dr. Lauren slowly rises to her feet, too, so we are eye to eye. She holds my gaze. I don't trust what she will say next, and I am ready to fight again as I have before.

"Jane? Is that you?" She plays dumb. I hate her so much. I hate her calmness, her thinking she can change me, Amy, and every other person who has walked into this God-forsaken room with her.

"Don't patronize me!" My voice gets louder each time I talk, a deliberate volume increase. I love turning it up and to the right.

She puts her hand up, signaling me to keep quiet. "Can you please lower your voice?" she asks quietly, in a voice a mother uses for her toddler.

"Why?" I whisper through gritted teeth. "Are you afraid you will be found out about what a fraud you are?" I am whisper-yelling, warning her that I can and *will* fly off the handle at any moment. My jaw is so tense, my whole body responds, and I feel a sharp pain in my uterus. *Poppy*, I think, grabbing my belly out of instinct. Dr. Lauren's eyes follow my hand, her eyes widening in shock and surprise.

"Are you pregnant, Jane?" *Why does she ask things that she already knows?*

"Stop playing dumb!" I yell at the top of my lungs, a switch turning on inside me.

"Ok, calm down. We can talk about it together." Her eyes stay steady on mine until she backs up, slowly lowering and grabbing the clipboard on the couch behind her. The name on the top of the paper reads *"London Rose."*

"No!" I scream again, reaching for one of the obnoxiously bright pillows on the floor and throwing it toward the clipboard. My aim has always been poor, and I miss hitting the pitcher of water instead, knocking it to the ground and breaking it with a crash.

"You will *not* hurt London, too!" I leap towards her, over the broken glass and puddle of water, desperate to grab the chart so she can't use it for harm. Dr. Lauren sees me coming, jumps left, and I fall with a thud on the couch. I am out of breath, lifeless, and defeated. The thud continues. A loud knock at the door pulls me out of the cushions, the room spinning upon standing. I see her go to the door, opening it slightly so the room is concealed.

"Hi, are you ok in there?" a male voice I recognize asks through the crack of the door.
*Is that Jake? What is he doing…*my mind races with a million questions as I reorient myself to the room: the pillows, the feather, the blankets, the tree, the *candle.*

"We are ok; I tripped and knocked over the glass pitcher. You know how clumsy I am." She answers him with a nervous laugh.

"Ok, Peggy, if you say so. Let me know if you need anything; I'm the push of a button away." She thanks him and clicks the door shut, her back facing me as she breathes deeply before turning around.

Peggy? Suddenly, the room is spinning, and I felt faint. The broken glass is on the floor before me, water everywhere. I am in between two worlds, two people, two *me's*. I feel crazy; the list of diagnoses and medications, the sessions, the underbreath discussion swirling around me, getting louder and louder. Suddenly, I see Jane next to me. I see her pain and feel the desire she has to burn it all down, to shut up the voices, and to start all over again.

"Jane can't protect everyone like she wants to. She is a failure." I shake back and forth, my tears coming out in uncontrollable sobs. The weight of her efforts coming out in waterfalls feels like both a release and a burden.

I can't bring myself to look at her but hear Peggy's soft footsteps cautiously approaching me. Her hand is on my shoulder, and she puts a box of tissues on my lap.

"London, are you back?" she asks sincerely, and I begin to feel safe again. And I have no idea how to answer her: I am here. But Amy and Jane are here too, and their voices have run the show so long that I can't recognize my own. I don't trust what just happened; I don't know how to switch from one part to the next, and I don't know who Jane is protecting. And then there is the issue of Dr. Lauren.

"I- I think so," I begin. Attempting to explain the in and out my brain is doing is almost impossible because I am nowhere near understanding it myself, but I try anyway.

"Jane scares me," I tell her. "When I saw her during the journey, she tried to burn the house down. She threw the candle, used the paints, and-"

Peggy interrupts me, "Let's slow down. Take a deep breath and start from the beginning."

"I am too afraid. Everything is upside down, and I can't-" The words escape me. My tongue feels heavy, and I can't speak. Peggy takes the cue and asks me to lie down, making a space under the table, as I saw Dr. Lauren do for Amy.

"You were there," I say out loud.

"What do you mean?" Peggy asks, smoothing out the blanket as I lay on top of it. She then sits at the top of the pillow.

"On my trip. Jane, Amy, and then you were there. I, or Jane and Amy, called you Dr. Lauren." I can't see her face, but all of her movement stops. Her hands touch my shoulders, her fingers cold as ice.

"Sometimes, people we encounter just before the journey can be helpers, sort of a metaphor in your psyche for those helping you along your journey." Her voice is at a higher octave than before. Her explanation makes sense for Jake, the boy who checked me in when I arrived but who also appeared during my psychedelic trip. But Dr. Lauren, she was different. She was as real as Amy and Jane but wasn't there to protect me. *She wasn't a part of me.*

"Maybe we should get to know Jane like we did for Amy," Peggy suggests, attempting to change the subject for a reason I can't quite understand. She continues, "Did something cause her to take over London?"

Thinking back, even ten minutes, is like digging through hot sand, all the grains falling back into the hole as soon as you dig it out. Everything is jumbled together, the lines of consciousness and unconsciousness blurred, the boundaries between me and the parts of me like particles that are experts in osmosis.

I recall sitting in the room with Peggy and getting in touch with Amy. I can remember accessing her and how she cooperated until she didn't, and that is when I realized Jane was in the room. The scene comes back to me vividly, and I remember using the restroom while Peggy slipped out into the hallway.

The tiny bathroom inside the room was only a tad bigger than the one in an airplane. I stood staring in the mirror for a long time, trying to make peace with the information about parts that I had just been told. The idea of a "good part" was foreign to me and my church upbringing; I was raised a good southern Baptist who believed in our eternal damnation since the minute we exited the womb. I searched my face in the tiny, plastic-like mirror, looking for the things that were Amy and Jane—and that which was me. Who was I, anyway? When I saw Amy and Jane, I knew their voices, but the thing the Journey gave me that I had yet to give voice to was *London*. I watched Amy, Jane, and Dr. Lauren act out their parts as a fly on the wall, a witness to it all. I was them, but I, London Rose, was *watching* them, apart from them. I don't recall the last time I, myself, was at the forefront. The worst part was that I didn't even know I had disappeared into the background.

Washing my hands, I exit the room and sit on the couch, only to find that Peggy hadn't returned. Getting settled on the couch, I adjusted the pillows, pulled the blanket up around my waist and waited. For the first time of my life, I felt separated from my anxiety, my OCD, my *Amy*. It was all new to me, but I was willing to explore it.

The door opened, and Peggy returned. It looked as though she had been running, her hair was disheveled, she was out of breath and her cheeks were pink. But the thing that gives heraway the most is her loose fitting, linen long sleeved shirt has been rolled up at the sleeves, and peeking out from underneath the fabric is a tattoo of a California Poppy.

My eyes fly open, desperate to hold on to this moment, with Peggy next to me, London trying to tell the story Jane has taken from her. I gulp for air, grabbing my chest, afraid that I will suffocate before I can get the words out.

"It's okay, London. Stay with me. You are safe. Your story is safe here. Your voice is safe here." Peggy repeats these words until I find my breath again, each one slower than the one before. When it is steady enough to speak, I dig up a memory that is so far buried that it hurts to recall.

"When I lost the baby," I pause. I need to take my time here. I need to hold on to the self, me, London. "Nothing in the delivery room was the same as when I gave birth to my son. The lights were off, and the room was dark. No one cheered, no baby cries echoing through the room." I recall the moment; it flooded back to me as if it was happening all over again. I can feel my uterus cramping, the way it did after the 48-hour labor the nurses had promised me would only take 8.

"She was still in the bag of water, and they cut it open with permission. And she was there, her flesh still young, and that's when we found out what had happened: her cord caught around her neck, strangling her." My throat tightens, and I feel the urge to stop, to bury it back in the rubble as I have all these years. But I stop. *You deserve to be heard, London,* a voice says.

It's Peggy.

"We left the hospital with nothing. One nurse ensured us we had her tiny footprints stamped on a piece of pink paper. They were no bigger than a penny. But we left empty-handed, returning to my son with no sibling." I am steady, reciting the story as I have many times before, but I stop. Facing a crossroads, wondering if it's safe to vocalize aloud.

"When I got home, I was alone but had to hold it all together. My husband worried about me; my son had so many questions. I couldn't sleep; my milk came in and took days to go down, and for months, I felt phantom kicks of her in my stomach. I missed her so much- her growing in my belly, missed what she would have been outside of the womb: a sister, a daughter, a ballerina, maybe." So many hopes and dreams that died the day she did. They don't tell you this about losing someone you love: you lose them, but you also lose everything you had hoped for them.

"We decided the best way for her to live on was to name her. We named her after my mother who had passed away when I was only 6 years old." The mention of yet another trauma, hangs in the air.

"We named her Poppy."

Her hands flee to her tattoo, covering the inked on her arm. She knows before I have to spell it out, "And that is what triggered Jane, wasn't it?"

I nod.

Jane told me she was pregnant," Peggy recalls the scene that unfolded before this one, piecing the puzzle together for me.

"Her rage makes so much sense now. Tell me, London, what did she do with all that anger when you met her on your journey?"

The vivid yellows, oranges, and reds are easy to recall. Her rage is building inside of me, and I can feel her in the heat that grows from the home my baby once had.

"She met Amy at this treehouse, and you were there too, but she didn't trust you. She said you were trying to hurt Amy, and you were obsessed with protecting a candle, which made her more mad. So she yelled and screamed at you both and took your candle and-"

Peggy finishes my sentence, "tried to burn it all down."

She's not asking me a question. The words are a statement of facts, telling the story as it unfolded. Her stare is blank. She looks past me to the table with the picture of a tree sitting on it.

I look behind me, seeing what she is seeing, catching her gaze again.

"How did you know that?" I said, my heart racing anxiously again.

Peggy stares back at me, her eyes wide, and I can hear our matching, thumping hearts.

"Because I was there."

33
Peggy

This week has been a blur. I was off my usual pattern of seeing clients as they came through because I asked Tom for a different rotation for the week. Without saying much, he understood that I needed to see a different side of the process. Client work is my favorite part of my job; I love watching the breakthrough, the magic of what it means to fall in love with yourself again, or for many, the first time.

But this morning, when I got into my old green Volvo, my insides matched the itchiness of the wool-blended seats. The tweed reminded me of a poet trapped inside the jacket of a finance guy; the elbows were the only part courageous enough to break through the stuffy fabric. I do everything I can to bring to mind a time when I was young and free, where my ghosts didn't follow me. The KuKui beads hanging from my rearview mirror get me there: I am back in Maui with my best friend, running in the early morning light, the whales jumping every other step, and the waves reminding me that things come and go. I rub the smooth surface of the beads through my fingers and then let them go, allowing them to sway back and forth as I start the car, which gives a little lurch.

Her protest of our excursion happens about every fifth time

I leave the house, which I rarely do unless I'm going to work. Today, I shouldn't be going to work. It's my day off, but I need to see Tom. I need to see if there is another door to unlock, another layer of magic to this job that I have yet to experience.

I have been running from my past life since I started at PCMI. The timing of the job coincided with my self-induced trauma, and I ran from one situation to the next. I come from a long line of psychotherapists; I saw firsthand how vital the work was. My mother and father were forerunners in their field and contributed large amounts of studies, papers, and work to further the field. So, although it was in the cards for me to follow suit, I also married someone who provided a different side of life: a farmer. Our life was a mixture of plants, soil, animals, cows, and then me, in my little office, seeing patients who needed deep healing. It's a tough job to hear the suffering of others and not carry it myself, an art that I am afraid I am still working on. The farm made it possible, though. The soil was my therapist, allowing me to till her, plant a seed of hope, and watch it grow. After a long day of seeing clients, I would go out to the garden, getting dirt beneath my fingernails and allowing the aroma of the herbs to meet me where I needed it. I saw firsthand how healing nature was, and I slowly began to dabble in the medicinal properties of plants.

We had our first child around this time, a tiny seed I birthed. I felt the gift the earth had given me, the interchange of planting and birthing inside me all over again. Little by little, the old me, who drove a green Volvo, held my parents' passion and dipped into the magical world of the garden, plants, and medicine, began to fade away. The all-consuming love for my new role as the mother took over, seen in metaphor by my cherished and reliable Volvo being used as a planter for non-native plants once it died. While I loved this out-of-the-box flower bed, I couldn't help but wonder at the symbol of it all: my old life making a home for an unnatural species.

Sometimes, we see our life in the mirror of the world, art, and the broken stove on Thanksgiving day. Life has a way of alerting us to the neglected parts inside. As our son grew, I felt more and more like this Volvo: broken, replaced, and holding everything that felt unnatural. I wasn't as good of a mother as I wanted to be; it wasn't a natural response for me like I heard others describe. I didn't know how to comfort him; the meals were entirely out of my range of skills, and pretend play felt like a slow death of boredom. I didn't hold the mom's guilt that I wasn't present enough; I had quit my job and was there for every milestone, first food, first rollover, steps, and first day of preschool. The guilt I held was that no matter how hard I tried, I felt like I wasn't fit for this role. I wasn't built with the right tools for the job.

One night, after a particularly challenging day of tantrums, food refusal, and nap defiance, something inside me broke. I lost it entirely and yelled and screamed at my little boy, his confused eyes staring straight back up at me. Once I started, I couldn't stop. I went through the kitchen and began throwing things at the wall: the yogurt on the counter, the half-full glass of wine, and even a stick of butter. I was in my world of releasing pent-up energy, unaware of the shrill-like screams from my son. At one point, I grabbed a handful of spoons that needed to be put away from the dishwasher and was ready to launch them across the room when I saw it: his terrified eyes, his petrified body, the tears streaking his red cheeks. I've seen enough clients whose mom or dad lost their tempers enough to know *this would stick*. Putting the spoons down, I ran over to him, trying to hug him and reassure him that I didn't mean it, that everything would be ok, that I was still the same mommy I was every other day.

Running to him, I reached out my arms to scoop him up and make it right again, but he did not come to me. Screaming, he ran away into his room and hid behind his crib. I followed him softly at first, hoping I could replace what he just saw with a smile and kind voice, but he screamed as I approached, burying himself into a ball in the corner of the room. The rage I experienced in the kitchen came flooding back, and I started yelling again; this time, it all pointed at him. I was angry that he needed what I couldn't give him, and although this wasn't his fault, I was so disappointed and angry at myself that I took it out on him. I got down on my knees at one point, pointing my finger in his face, saying a bunch of angry words that I don't recall, and that's when I saw it: the little light he once held in his eyes was gone. His bright, blue eyes, with the flicker of joy, hope, and innocence that only childhood can hold, were now glazed over, the light gone.

The extinguishing of joy stopped me in my tracks. It was all my fault. I had taken something from him that no amount of hugs, kisses, balloons, or vacations to the Grand Canyon could replace. We made a core memory here, and I knew he would be reminded each time he saw me. But what was worse was that I *liked* how the screaming and yelling felt. It woke something up inside me, and the day-to-day, mundane life would not allow the space to find out what it was.

Over the next few days, I went through the motions, pretending nothing happened. I tried to speak to him as much as a four-year-old could understand. I confessed it to my husband, who was kind but firm; we would not be a house that yelled at our children. His childhood was tumultuous and full of never-resolved fights, which he did not want our son to experience. I agreed, but doing so felt like I was shoving something down that wanted to get out. I tried every tool I had in my box, but nothing worked. I raged more and more, not necessarily because I was mad, but because to do so felt *so good*. In hindsight, I am unsure how long I lasted before I couldn't anymore. The timeline is about a month, but it was boiling for so many years even before that, before my son, too. I never had the tools I needed for the job before me: I wasn't cut out for marriage either. His family didn't understand me, a black sheep of woo-woo therapeutic and Buddhist ideologies in the middle of the white, Protestant herd. I hated housework; everything was a mess, which irritated him even if he had never said it. The laundry was in the bin at all times, something I still adhere to; why *fold it if we are just going to wear it again?* And so, one night, staring at the basket of clothes I knew needed folding, I dumped it into a suitcase and zipped it up.

I left a note on the counter that said, "Getting milk!" and slipped out the back door, walking the three miles to town. It was for the best that I wasn't coming back; I was not and could not be the wife, mother, or woman that they wanted me to be. So, I left that night and never went back.

I've made an okay life despite the guttural pain of regret I live with daily. The only thing that has taken off the edge and allowed little trickles of forgiveness is microdosing. When I started at PCMI, I microdosed here and there as part of "research." No one knew my past life, the son and husband who wondered if I would ever return with a gallon of milk. Whenever I walked into the office, I felt like I was wearing a wig and oversized glasses in a feeble attempt to be a new person. But so far, it's worked; the psilocybin has given me space to love and forgive myself, attempt to put it behind me, and live an everyday life again.

At the time I started at PCMI, psilocybin was illegal in California, but now it's decriminalized, so microdosing has become more accessible as time has gone on. Today, I am on a new mission: find Tom at the lab and ask him to participate in whatever research they are doing. As I drive into work, I am taken aback by the beauty of the sea and the waves that never cease. The sparkling waters and the ocean breeze offer me some breathing space that, even after thirty years, is rare air. *He will be 33 this year,* I think.

The lab at PCMI is a small room in which different types of psychedelic mushrooms are tested and put into various forms in an attempt to see if the method by which one is taking the drug affects the drug itself. It shouldn't, but you'd be surprised by the mental game that one can play when it comes to a fungus vs. a piece of chocolate. Earlier this week, I ventured to find Tom, but I checked the lab when he wasn't at his office. It was earlier in the morning, and I had tried to time it just right so there wouldn't be a crowd. And when I arrived, it looked like I was in the clear. The thing about Tom is that even if there are a hundred people in the room, he makes you feel like you are the only one.

"Hi, Tom," I say to him before seeing him. He is leaning down, his face in the cupboards, undoubtedly looking for an ingredient that he was told to find. Tom loves to experiment, and some of his findings have been our greatest breakthroughs at PCMI.

"Hello, Peggy!" His voice is boisterous; no one I know is this happy at work. I can't help but smile back at him. "I know, it's my day off. Are you surprised to see me?"

"Don't tell me you have gotten in the habit of taking the mushrooms for yourself." He grins with a smirk…and a wink. *Does he know?* I haven't been doing anything illegal but haven't told anyone. If anyone is safe sourcing and taking psilocybin, it's me. I know the pitfalls and dangers in and out.

"I solemnly swear that I still have yet to try our recipe." I smile, holding up three fingers in a scout's honor.

"Why is that?" he asks, his smile fading slightly. I honestly don't know why he is taking this personally.

"I-I don't know, Tom," I begin, instantly regretting entertaining my gut feelings and thus needing to come down here on a Tuesday when Tom decides we should exchange feelings.

"Say no more." He says, holding up his hand in a stop motion. "I get it. I have a past I want to forget, too." He picks up another tray of mushrooms, scribbling something I can't make out from his chicken scratch. Placing it down, he rests his muscular and worn-out forearms on the edge of the metal counter, looking me straight in the eyes. His are soft, his voice lowered and genuine, "I broke my number one rule, Lauren. I got into my colleagues' business, and I shouldn't have. I hope you'll forgive me."

"Oh, Tom! It's going to take a lot more than that to scare me off," I say jokingly, trying to ease the tension my body has latched on to.

He smiles, letting the whole thing go, "What can I help you with today, Peggy?"

"Well, it looks like you aren't the only one breaking rules, Tom," I say, wringing out my wrists. I offer some personal anecdotes on his behalf, which are also strange to me. Even though his prying questions agitated me, they riled up my nervous system, and I enjoyed it. I can't remember the last time someone asked anything about me, even if it was only three words.

I continue, "I don't have another client for three days, and I'd like to see what is done here for a change."

Much like the lake, Tom's eyes glitter with mischief and

delight.

"Ah, I see. So you want to make something different?"

"Yes. The giant mushrooms that our usual, career-driven city boy likes to just take a bite out of don't seem like it will be this next round's flavor if you know what I mean. We are dealing with women diagnosed with general anxiety disorder, so something more palpable, maybe?"

Tom raises a finger and quickly slips behind the double swinging doors, leaving me to stand in a sea of mushrooms, microscopes, and lab equipment, hoping no one will come and ask me questions about what each one does.

I wait about five minutes when it starts to rain, the sound calming on the roof above us. A small group of scientists enters, muttering to one another and looking at their carts, and I stand with them, shoulder to shoulder with one another and the mushrooms. Standing right next to me is Emily, a mom with a toddler who she undoubtedly takes on long walks in the stroller, and an older woman who adorns a hand-dyed scarf around her neck with a tiny dog brooch keeping it in place. As someone is about to make small talk, Tom returns from the back, sweat dripping off his forehead.

"Oh, hello. Can I offer anyone a sample?" Everyone laughs because they know he is joking, but I am not. I would quickly eat a mushroom right out of that box.

"Excuse me," I say, trying to slink past the older woman and her happy dog brooch so I can finish my conversation with Tom and get started. There are too many people in way too close proximity for me.

He pulls me to the side and says in a low voice, "Peggy, I'm so sorry. I don't have what I thought I did, and even if I did, we can't create something new and then test it blindly on the next set of applicants. We have a schedule, and the last Sunday of the month is the only day we can start a new formula."

Damn. My face falls, and it is the first time in a long time that I feel nervous and unprepared for the next round of applicants. I picture one of them, London's Zoom call, that contagious laugh, and something inside of me wants this experience to be great for her.

"Could I come to your house and get them?" I can't believe I asked him that, and from the looks of it, he can't either, and for the first time in three years, he stammers on his words, "Uh-um-um sure. How about you meet me at my house in about an hour?" He writes down his address and hands it to me. Taking it, I shove it into my pocket, nod in agreement, and run out into the rainstorm.

***

Tom's house is nothing I had thought it would be—if I had ever considered this and what his house would be like in the many years of knowing him. Tucked at the end of a long driveway covered by trees, his house boasted nothing but charm. This little cottage was feminine and adorable for a man who lives alone: painted a delicate yellow with white trim, a red door, and a white picket fence with flowers lining the outside perimeter.

Gaging myself with one last look in the mirror, I approach the front door. He opens it before I can knock.

"Peggy! Come on in." He is out of breath.

Hesitantly but also overcome with curiosity, I step inside a bright, open-concept living area. It is bohemian, shabby chic. I gasp when I see the white canvas couch with a million pillows that seemed like you could sink right in and never get up again. Everything in the house is the opposite aesthetic Tom presents himself as.

"I know. It's not what you pictured, is it?" He chuckles behind me, shutting the door quietly.

"My, uh, sister decorated it for me. She's one of those big fancy designers out in Los Angeles, and she showed up one weekend with her entire crew and said I'd be doing her a favor if I let her decorate it for me."

"It's gorgeous!" I gush. The walls, divided into two sections, make the room feel roomier than it is. The bottom half has wainscoting, and the top half has baby blue and white stripes going up the walls and onto the ceiling. A large chandelier hangs in the middle of the room.

"Where did you get that?" I ask, pointing to the big wooden box hanging from the ceiling with large gold chains. From the center of the box were mason jars of multiple shapes, sizes, and lengths, the innermost core lit up by lightbulbs on the inside.

"Oh," Tom said with a grin. "I made that."

I turn to stare at him, my mouth hanging open despite my futile attempts to keep it shut. "And here I thought you only knew about mushrooms," I say, diverting my eyes as soon as they lock with his.

"About that. I am sorry about earlier. I don't tell people I grow mushrooms, and I didn't know that you knew either, but I'm glad you're here." Tom mumbles as he walks out of the room, and I suppose I should follow.

He meanders past his kitchen (navy blue cabinets and gold fixtures) and dining room (with a gorgeous, circular table that I assume he also made) and into a hallway with a door at the edge. As he walks, he flips a switch that turns on the wall scones, which look like outside street lamps with a retro lightbulb inside each one.

Remind me to get his sister's number.

Tom opens the door and steps down twice into a musty, somewhat predictable garage for what I expected Tom's house to be. It is dark, except for one bulb hanging with a giant string, which turns on once you pull on it. And that he does. The small light-flow reveals two tennis balls hanging from the ceiling to let drivers know when to stop their car as they enter. Tom's truck is out front.

"Oh, sorry. I'm not used to having anyone else here. It must feel dark and stuffy." *Is he nervous?* He presses the garage door button, and the door slowly opens, creaking the whole way up.

"Ah ha!" Tom shouts and holds up a gardening tool I have never seen before. "Follow me," he says as he opens a door that leads into the famous mushroom garden.

The minute I step through the door, I am Alice in Wonderland. Vines crawl up the side of the house, and the mushroom garden is more extensive than I ever imagined. "How many acres is this?" I ask, my mouth hanging open for the second, or was it third, time?

"The lot I own is three acres. But my mushrooms only take up half an acre." He smiles, waving his hand flippantly into the vast green in front of him. I admit my tree house brings spooky vibes, but it is also unique and could be charming had I had a decorator sister who needed a favor. But this? This was amazing. Tom has land for what seemed like days and the views! The views are so beautiful they almost seem fake. As far as the eye can see, brush covers the mountains like a blanket, tucked in every twist and drop and uphill, like I used to tuck my son in bed at night. *Snug as a bug in a rug!* All the trees came to a point to meet the base of mountains shaded in various purples and blues.

"You should see them in late summer. The sunset never

ends." Tom is beside me; I feel his arm brush mine; if I wanted, I could extend my fingers to touch his. But I don't. Want to, that is.

I close my eyes and imagine what that must be like— purples, pinks, oranges, and yellows, all in a watercolor masterpiece. Then I open them again.

"She's leaving us, you know," I say, pointing at the *almost* full moon rising in the sky.

"Who is?" Tom asks, hand covering his eyes to search the horizon for someone I see, but he doesn't.

"The moon. 8 cm every year. Pretty soon, she will be out of our orbit, and all we will be left with is the sun."

"Says *who*?!" Tom bellows with bewilderment.

"The scientists, that's *who!*" I smile back, playfully pushing his shoulder.

"Never put too much stock in science, Peggy. You gotta *feel* it to know it."

"Spoken like a true peddler of psychedelics," I say, folding my arms across my chest. I could stay here, looking at this view, talking to him all night.

"Ah, come on now. Psychedelics is science." He begins to meander again, this time through the rows of mushrooms. I follow, careful not to step on any of the budding spores.

"The science is in the soil. Whatever soil it's grown in creates the magic it holds." He bends down to a plot of smaller mushrooms, which I recognize as the ones we usually use at the lab. I bend down, too.

"This soil, it's the best stuff there is. It's been regeneratively grown and packed with nutrients. It's the only soil that I will grow my psilocybin in."

"How did you get it here?" I ask if he is telling me the truth or has decided to pull one over on me.

"It took me three years to tend to the land," he says, a sorrow hanging in the corners of his words that I can't quite place.

"Of course you did. That makes perfect sense: that you, the mushroom man, who lives in a Southern Living magazine set against the backdrop of every California calendar, took three years to make the perfect soil." There goes my mouth, hanging open again.

He stands up abruptly, mushrooms in hand, and walks back toward the garage. We lock eyes, and for the first time in a long time, I feel a deep connection of empathy and understanding with someone other than my clients.

"As you said back at the lab, *I have a past I want to forget, too*," I say. He sticks out his hand, and we shake on it. Our hands remain clasped together in mid-air for awkwardly longer than they should, only to be interrupted by my phone alarm ringing.

Oh shit. The candle.

"You got somewhere to be?" Tom asks, heading back into the garage. "Uh, no," I stammer. "I just need to get back and feed my cat, Theo." I am wringing my wrists again—a nervous habit. I have never been away from the candle for this long; it is a practice that I hold very religious to. Of course, it's for fire safety, but somewhere deep down inside of me, I also believe it somehow is righting the wrongs of my past, a hope that the light has returned to my son's soul. But this will only happen as long as the flame keeps on burning. *What would I do, and how would I go on if it blew out?*

"I was going to offer you a cup of tea or pint of beer while I put these in the dehydrator…" he trails off, placing the mushrooms inside a giant white box with knobs and buttons and lights.

"Tom," I say, more agitated than I want to, "this seems like the same psilocybin we always use. Is this going to be worth it or what?" My cheeks are hot, and I feel embarrassed from lashing out at him like this. His face falls.

"It's ok, go on. I can bring them to you when I'm done. You're in that treehouse at the top of the hill, right?"

"Yeah!" I scream, my head already out the window of my car, and I am peeling away, dirt clouding up behind me, covering Tom, standing in his driveway, hurt and confused.

That makes two of us.

34
London

"It *is* you." I stare at her, noticing what I hadn't before: the way her gray curls swirl around her forehead, the wrinkles that delicately have begun to appear, and the unforgettable kindness that lives in her eyes.

"Where are your scars?" I ask, my fingers instinctually reaching out to touch her face.

"What scars?" She shies away from me. Both bewildered, we sit, trying to understand what happened.

"On my journey, you were there, but your name wasn't Dr. Peggy, you were Dr. Lauren and-"

"-Lauren" was my married name." Her voice a quiet whisper, as she looks down at her hands, twirling a ring in a circle on her left finger. I wait. Not on either side of consciousness did I know about her marital status, but her use of the word "was" tells me there is a story of pain buried somewhere inside.

"You had all these scars, all over your face. They looked like burn marks, and one was fresh, an open wound almost. But, they aren't there now," I marvel at the miraculous healing that from my experience, took place. Peggy closes her eyes, taking in everything I am saying, and without opening them, she says, "What else was I like?"

"I didn't trust you. I thought you were taking advantage of Amy." My voice trails off as I begin to put together the pieces. Processing out loud, I continue, "Amy is a part of me who protects the version of me-"

"It's called an *exile*. When a trauma happens and a part of you stays stuck, they become an exile. The version of you that existed when your house burned down became exiled as a result of the trauma." She still isn't looking at me, her mind a million other places than this room.

"Ok, so Amy protected the exiled part of me. She came to you for a psychedelic trip," I begin, waiting to see if Peggy is tracking with me. She smiles, "Sounds familiar, doesn't it?"

"But then Jane comes to see Amy because she is pregnant and the doctor said she wasn't, so she shows up and-"

"Wait, wait, wait. Slow down. If we are going to do this, let's dig in and do it." Peggy arises, grabs the candle on the table and sits it down between us.

"I started working at PCMI 30 years ago. After my first year on the job, I knew this was the work that I was meant to do. But it came at a cost for me. When I was about to be in charge of my first participant, I lit a candle the night before honoring the work and honoring the client's fire within. I vowed to never take away someone's light like I did to people I loved." She pauses, a whole story is in that sentence, but she doesn't fill in the blanks. I don't need to know every detail to honor her journey.

"That flame I lit, twenty-nine years ago, is still this flame. I've never let it blow out, carefully transferring it from wick to wick, driving slower than the limit with my hazard lights on day after day as I bring it to work and back." Her voice is a mixture of proud and embarrassed, like she can't decide which one she should feel about it. I scoot back out of fear my breath will blow it out, and it dances with the air from my moving body.

"It's ok," she says. "The flame is so resilient. If there's one thing I've learned doing this work for 30 years it's that flames rarely can actually be blown out. Even when they aren't there, they are waiting in the wings, ready to ignite and spontaneously combust as soon as the conditions are right. And that's why I love this plant medicine. It has a way of making the conditions exactly right." We are both staring at the flame, and I see it differently than I've ever seen a candle before. I see it dancing; I see it standing still. I see its potential, the will to live and to dream, the ability to jump from home to home, holding vigil for the hundreds of participants like myself who have walked into this room. But also, Peggy. She *is* the candle, witnessing the lost and hurting souls that sit before her. She is the beacon of hope, the reason people can find healing.

"So, Jane, we never did find out who she is protecting," she makes it about me again.

"Can I try?" I ask, feeling more in touch with myself than I have since a very young age. Peggy looks pleasantly surprised. "Yes! Please," she says, her smile expanding wide across her face.

"When I met Jane, she was young and pregnant. But no one believed her, not even the doctor. She didn't have a husband; her mother had died, so she was nervous about being a mother herself, which drew her to Amy." Peggy nods for me to continue.

"Amy mothered her." I stop, not able to deduce things any further. *Why did Jane get upset with Dr. Lauren? Why didn't she let Amy mother her at that moment?* Shrugging my shoulders, I admit I don't know how the dots connect.

Peggy draws me back to the questioning we used for Amy.

"You are so close, London. Let me ask you this before you worry about why Jane did what she did or why she didn't like the Dr. Lauren part of me: ask who she is protecting." I close my eyes, a little afraid to ask her, worried she may come out again, taking over the situation. I am struggling to find her now, all I hear is Amy, anxiously ratting on about how to protect me in this moment, from the candle and from Jane. Sensing my struggle, Peggy offers something else to try, "Ask Amy to leave the room for a minute," she says.

And so I do. Amy protests, but I quietly guide her into a room with a window, so she knows I am there. And then I wait. My mind is quiet, a delightful yet uncomfortable feeling. I am not anxious, I am not worrying about something, about *anything*. I, London, am in the room, alone. The silence is so welcome, and I begin to enjoy this glimpse of who I am. And that is exactly when I sense her. Jane is here, although I can't see her, I know she is here because the room is suddenly getting hotter.

"Hi," I say in my head to her. She responds with a smaller hello, and I know immediately she thinks she's in trouble. I start with the two questions I remember we started with for Amy: "Who are you protecting?" and "How old do you think I am?" Her answers aren't so much surprising as they are absolutely gut wrenching. My heart sinks when I hear her, my whole body melting in defeat.

"She said she's protecting me, when my mother died." I weep, remembering what it was like to have my mom there and then she just wasn't.

"My dad didn't tell me how she died, so I have lived my whole life not knowing." Saying it aloud makes it so much worse than I ever thought it was.

"When something happens we don't get answers on, our

mind automatically tries to make up stories as to why that something has happened. That is your mind's way of making sense of things that make no sense at all. Although a poor substitute for the truth, it gave you a foundation of security."

"But that doesn't make sense, Jane being pregnant doesn't have anything to do with me losing my mom."

"Ask her again," Peggy insists.

Jane speaks to me again and when she tells me the rest of her story, of how she came to be, I don't see an angry, crazy person anymore. I see a human who is badly hurt in a cycle of life and death of mother and child entanglement that she couldn't escape.

"She says she had to emerge because Amy wasn't doing her job." I explain with some hesitation. This doesn't fit what Peggy told me.

"Ah, yes. Amy is what we call a *manager*, she is there to protect the exile. But when a manager isn't doing her job, another part will emerge, and we call these parts 'firefighters.'" I raise my eyebrows at her, a crooked smile on my face. "That's ironic," I say, and we share a comedic break in the heavy atmosphere.

"These are the parts that go into emergency mode. For Jane, Amy has been at work for a long time, but still couldn't protect you from your mother dying *or* your baby dying. Those deep, deep traumas coupled with the years of misdiagnoses and gaslighting by your former therapists, being in a room with me triggered a last ditch effort to protect you." Peggy explains with caution, saving room for me to make the story my own.

Jane, is this true?

"She's both the mother I didn't get to have and the daughter I lost. Her rage is the fire of a mom who goes to any length to protect her child, and her baby is the small spark that forever lives inside my womb." The air in the room goes stale and even the candle stops moving. There is something about the truth of this that Peggy and I both feel to our core. Our wounds circle around each other, a oneness between our losses in childhood and motherhood that have come colliding together like the particles and gasses that make up the fire that sits between us.

She speaks first.

"There is a Buddhist teaching called 'The Bejeweled Net of Indra" and it says that when the world was made, there was a large net that had a jewel at every vertex and every jewel reflected every other jewel around it. It teaches we are multifaceted creatures, but we are all one. My pain is your pain and your pain is mine, too. London, I broke protocol before you went on your trip. I microdosed a new type of mushroom that I shouldn't have done before the session. It's against the ethics of what I do, not to mention the agreement I signed thirty years ago." She looks disappointed in herself, and while I am not trained in psychotherapy, I am thoroughly well versed in being a broken human with parts who do things we don't want to do. I take the lead.

"My pain is your pain, right? I understand why you did it." I take her hands, and we hold them together, floating over the warmth of the candle.

"You do?" She asks and I see that she isn't even sure herself.

"You knew all my history before I came into this room. You read my chart and you interviewed me yourself. Whatever part Dr. Lauren is, she needed Amy and Jane to find *Peggy* again."

It's her turn to cry and she does, softly at first, followed by sobs, her hands leaving mine to wipe her tears.

"My scars, the ones you saw on Dr. Lauren's face? Those are the scars of all my participants I haven't saved. Every time their trip doesn't "work" or they leave here not all integrated, I internalize it. So when I saw your application, the mirrors of my pain reflected back to me, your many years of finding no help at the end of the road; I was desperate for this to be the answer, like if you could find healing, then maybe, it would make up for the ones I couldn't save. Including my husband and son." Her vulnerability catches me off guard, and her humanity is stunning. I see the jewel in her, shining and reflecting, and I feel her rays of light connect to the one inside me, too.

"Is that why you were so protective of the candle?" I ask, pulling my knees into my chest.

"I don't know who I am if I am not saving someone, and the candle is every soul I have helped and the ones I haven't. I have held onto the hope that the light I put out in my son can somehow heal back into a flame if I keep this lit long enough. But Jane? She saw it for the jail it was-"

"In both you and me," I say, somberly. Here we were, two women, living in cages of ceremony, ritual, guilt and grief, each allowing the lights of our womb space, the seat of identity and intuition, that were first extinguished long ago, to stay unlit. And somehow, in the realm of the unconscious, our beautiful parts met, playing out the bad roles that they had been forced into, so we could find ourselves once again.

Lifting up the candle that sits between us, Peggy begins a dedication:

"To Jane. Who came to save us both, a true firefighter, who knew the only prescription either of us needed was a controlled burn. She had no other choice besides burning the whole fucking thing down." Lowering the candle, she locks her eyes with mine, holding up her fingers..1..2..3, and together we blow out the flame. The cell doors open, and after a 30 year sentence, we are finally free.

"Hello, *London*." Peggy looks at me, extending her hand.

"Hello, *Peggy*" I respond, shaking it.

We meet each other, and ourselves, for the very first time.

35
Fire

An ancient myth says that when a candle is blown out, the energy of the flames never really leaves. Our power, our purpose, the thing we were initially lit for, cycles back into the inhale of the ones that blew us out.

The purposeful exhales of these two beautiful souls, an Exodus from that which has trapped them, pushed my own breath right out of my fiery lungs, and as fast as the spark that lit me ran out, all my light ran out.

As my smoke rose, swirling white in the dark room, they inhaled their power back into the Self. I travel as potential, into the nose down to the womb space like a glittering waterway that can not be destroyed. I settle there, healing the wounds that have lived there too long. I soften the walls of the womb, and I make a home there. I no longer live outside of them but am now seated on the throne of dreams, of divinity, of birthing new and beautiful things into the world.

I see a candle right there in the middle. The wick is bending over brittle, and the wax is hard and cold. I approach. I hover. I wait.

Hello London.

Hello Peggy.

Their voices rattle the bones; like an earthquake, a flash of heat jolts through the womb space. It's enough for me, and I light the wick, the sparkling and crackling cheering on the will to be lit, burn, and thrive.

36
Peggy

I died a tiny death that day when I blew out the candle. For thirty years, I've been afflicted by not knowing, and it served as a barrier to the pain I felt. I was obsessed with the "if only," and it kept me going strangely. I knew I couldn't continue, and Jane did too. That part of me started a slow death that day, one that took months to die out fully. But it also started the re-birth process, a natural and beautiful element of Buddhism I've long studied. I always thought it would only happen when my life ended, but because of my multiple parts, I've gotten to experience samsara many times in my life.

My re-birth is still in process. It's been six months since I met London and left PCMI. That session ended everything for me: my quest to save others and the incessant grudge I held against myself.   I am so grateful for the thirty years I had caged because it taught me how to be free.

I leave the house more and drive at the speed limit. I don't have a candle to care for except the one inside myself. I am meeting myself for the first time in a long time, and getting to know her is awkward, complex, and beautiful. There are days when I feel completely worthless without the contributions I'm making to the field of science in breakthrough studies. I went from writing the papers to being a footnote.

The first few months were occupied by an internal state of freeze. I still needed to unpack what needed to be corrected with my work, separating it from what felt right. I still believed this was the work I wanted to do, but I needed to do it my way. I've read numerous studies of therapy-assisted psychedelics, and when the client can process them, life-changing shifts can happen.

I never asked London to fill out the survey on the iPad that day. I couldn't bring myself to do it. What happened to her and me that day was beyond a study on a blue-lit screen; it felt almost sacrilegious to force it on her. I was flagged for incomplete data, but when Tom called me to discuss it, I had already written and prepared my resignation. But this was a turning point for me. As the days passed and I had space from PCMI and all that played a role in my identity, I realized that integration was the thing that was missing.

I, myself, am a product of this. Microdosing is good, but it can be great if I integrate my experiences. Dr. Lauren was left on an island for so long, begging Peggy to help her, to hear her and see her. Desperately trying to protect her. So, I've started therapy again, and with the decriminalization of psilocybin in California, I can continue my practice in a way that is right for me. Tom has been an enormous help, gracefully giving me space while teaching me all he knows about the mushrooms he grows.

Over the months, I've contemplated contacting my son. I found out from a Google search that his dad has remarried, and they live in Wyoming, which makes me smile. I'm glad he restarted, that he found a big, open space to live out the life he wants. My son, thirty-three now, lives only about 5 miles from me. I don't know if it's better to let things lie or to call him and try to reconcile. I have to decide if opening this door would benefit him or me. Sometimes, doors are better left shut. When I think of another fifty years without him, Dr. Lauren gets loud. She wants me to take this pain on again, to cage and punish myself and begs me not to call him. She seems to think that the only way I can soothe my pain is to force myself to cling to these old wounds.

I have learned to thank her for her mothering instincts, to honor the desire to care for him, which will always be there, and to remind her that caring and loving him does not include hurting myself. It's a daily battle, but I take it one day at a time, like an addiction that requires surrendering one day at a time. Today, I will not call. Today, I will garden, I will journal, I will take a walk, and I will do everyday things like go to the grocery store. Maybe I will call Tom and see if he wants to visit an art gallery. Yes, today calls for art.

37

London

She walks into my gallery, and I recognize her before she sees me. She must not know this: the art is all mine. I smile, hiding behind one of the weight-bearing beams in the middle of the gallery. I want to watch her and see what she does, which paintings catch her eye, and if any of them remind her of me.

She meanders through the rooms full of my work; some framed, some large, others bare and small. It's a quiet day at the gallery, and while I am usually at my studio painting, I stepped in for my assistant who needed a day off. I welcomed the chance to be around my own brush strokes; the ones that tell the story better than I could ever put into words.

My psychedelic experience was life-changing. The wounds it undid and the discovery of the self saved me from a place of darkness that I lived in for a long, long time. In some ways, because I had made my home there for many years, coming out into the light was disorienting. Coming home to my husband and my kids was not the sweet reunion that I thought it would be. Before going to PCMI, I had high hopes that I would return with a different story to write; a tale of a whole human being where all that afflicted me was behind me. I thought I would no longer yell, I wouldn't obsess over my kids bodies or ailments, my past or my future. I also thought that everyone would be as enlightened as me. But what greeted me when I returned were three human beings having a very human experience. And I, I greeted them with London for the first time, Amy and Jane waiting in the wings, a little upset that their voices weren't the loudest anymore. Which, of course, meant in those first few months back, they often reared their heads, like a child who throws a tantrum when they aren't getting enough attention.

I found an Internal Family Systems therapist who helps me work through the multiple parts of me, and reassign Jane and Amy to new, helpful roles. I learned that I don't want to banish either of them, that at their core, they loved me when I could not. Amy's obsession with detail and Jane's healthy fire have a new place in me: my art.

I began painting a few months after my trip. I found another guide who helped me with microdosing and as I got in touch with my parts and path again, I looked to all the expressions of self that I put away a long time ago. When I was in high school, I almost applied to art school and painting was one of the ways I coped with my pain, although I didn't know it then. During one of my microdosing sessions, I was at the beach and everything looked like a painting. The thing that struck me was the humanity involved in every brush stroke. It was in the Indra's Net that Peggy had told me about: everything was connected, it was all one. What if my pain could only transform when I worked with it instead of against it?

I went home that day, brought out the canvases and paints I had stored away in the attic and began. I painted day and night, the brushstrokes and colors transforming the darkest parts of me into beauty. I took classes, I used Amy to help me be patient and obsessive over color choices and details that would otherwise go unnoticed. She saw things in a multi-dimensional way, tapping me on the shoulder to take a closer look when I missed a streak of white or left out a hint of blue. I used Jane to fight for me, to remind me that this dream, this love, was worth pursuing. She spoke up when I wanted to freeze, when I felt selfish and ridiculous. She taught me to birth something new.

I opened the gallery only a few months ago; a strange thing to be an unknown artist who owns a gallery of nothing but her own work. This is what it's like to be London. I look around at the small and simple life I lead: I do the lunches, I paint, I play board games, I do yoga, and I am learning to love it all. There is a Buddhist koan I've latched on to that says "Ordinary mind is the Way." London, it turns out, is very ordinary. She has depths and multitudes, but at her core, she loves the mundane. Amy often tries to reject this, but I remind her that when we met on the journey, she wanted to escape and go to London. What if she never really wanted to go to the city but just yearned to meet *me?*

"Peggy." I say it more of a prayer than a statement. She tilts her head in my direction as I step out from behind the wooden pillar. Her eyes widen, her hand coming to her mouth as if life is just one giant surprise. We hug, holding tightly, not worried about the protocol to let go. Embracing her is like embracing myself. I feel my womb space flutter, an other-worldly reflex to our meeting in the unconscious.

"What are you doing here?" she asks, surprised, as Tom walks up next to her.

"You remember Tom, right?" her cheeks are pink, and I think she might be happy and at peace.

"Hi, of course I do." I smile at him and feel as if I am watching young love blossom. I look back at Peggy, and with pride, I answer her question, "I own this gallery, and all this art is mine." Her eyes well up with tears, and she looks in awe at the paintings around her again. Her eyes wander from piece to piece, landing on the large, full-length one in the back room. Tom shrinks back, knowing we need a moment to stare at what is in front of us: a woman with multiple heads and faces, her naked body exposed for all to see. But right below her navel, you see inside her womb space where a candle sits in the middle of her uterus, and two mushrooms float where her ovaries should be. She gasps, and I stand beside her, reaching for her hand. Our fingers interlace; her pain is my pain, and my healing is hers, too.

Appendix

What are psychedelics?

"The term *psychedelic* was coined in 1956 by the psychiatrist Humphry Osmond to describe the effects of drugs like LSD and mescaline. Osmond chose the Greek *psykhē* for "mind" and *dēloun* for "show," translating this new term as "mind manifesting." Another term for this class of substances, *entheogen*, was coined in 1979 and connotes spiritual intention or effects. The older term *hallucinogen* is still found in some laws and scientific literature.

There are hundreds of psychedelic compounds, and cataloging them is an ever-evolving process. Some of them occur naturally; others are created in the lab. The late chemist Alexander "Sasha" Shulgin estimated he created nearly two hundred new psychedelics, including 2C-B and 2C-T-7, which are phenethylamines, in the same category of chemical structures as mescaline and MDMA.

Classic psychedelics are grouped together because they all work on serotonin 2A receptors in the brain and central nervous system. Some studies suggest these compounds decrease blood flow to certain brain regions, including the default-mode network, a group of brain regions associated with higher-order metacognition, the construction of the ego, and conceptions of the self.

While conditions like depression and anxiety can reduce functional connectivity between certain brain regions, some research suggests that classic psychedelics can help temporarily rewire the brain and promote neuroplasticity by increasing and strengthening those connections. Several of these substances, including ayahuasca and mescaline, are naturally occurring and have been used as medicines and in spiritual practices for millennia."

UC Berkeley Center for the Science of Psychedelics, 2024

Psilocybin

Indigenous communities in Mexico and Central America have used **psilocybin-containing mushrooms** in celebrations, healing rituals, and religious ceremonies for millennia. In the 1950s and '60s, psychiatrists investigated the **therapeutic potential** of psilocybin, though less extensively than LSD. In the United States, most human psychedelic research halted in 1971 after President Nixon's Controlled Substances Act—Title II of the Comprehensive Drug Abuse Prevention and Control Act of 1970—went into effect, designating psilocybin as a Schedule I drug.

In 2000, researchers at Johns Hopkins University received federal and institutional approvals to give psilocybin to human volunteers who had never taken a psychedelic, leading to the landmark 2006 publication "**Psilocybin Can Occasion Mystical-type Experiences Having Substantial and Sustained Personal Meaning and Spiritual Significance**."

Like other classic psychedelics, psilocybin can cause visual and auditory distortions or changes; hypersensitivity to touch, light, and sound; an altered or slowed perception of time; and synesthesia.

(UC Berkeley Center for the Science of Psychedelics, 2023)

Is it legal?

Also known as psychotomimetics, hallucinogens, or psychedelics, entheogens are psychoactive substances that induce profound changes in perception. The word "entheogen" comes from the ancient Greek "entheos" for "divine," and "genesthai" for "generate," and refers to a connection with the inner divine; it's commonly used when the substances are taken with spiritual intent or when they have spiritual effects.

"Entheogen" is the preferred term of the Decriminalize Nature movement, which aims to change laws against "entheogenic plants and fungi" or to deprioritize enforcement of those laws. It has effectively done so in a growing number of U.S. cities.

(UC Berkeley Center for the Science of Psychedelics, 2024b)

The guide

Yet researchers believe it is not the molecules by themselves that can help patients change their minds. The role of the guide is crucial. People under the influence of psychedelics are extraordinarily suggestible — "think of placebos on rocket boosters," a Hopkins researcher told me — with the psychedelic experience profoundly affected by "set" and "setting" — that is, by the volunteer's interior and exterior environments. For that reason, treatment sessions typically take place in a cozy room and always in the company of trained guides. The guides prepare volunteers for the journey to come, sit by them for the duration and then, usually on the day after a session, help them to "integrate," or make sense of, the experience and put it to good use in changing their lives. The work is typically referred to as "psychedelic therapy," but it would be more accurate to call it "psychedelic-assisted psychotherapy."

—Pollan, M. (2024, April 2). My Adventures with the Trip Doctors - Michael Pollan. Michael Pollan. michaelpollan.com

Oneness

Many psychedelics users report mystical experiences, particularly in high-dose sessions. Some studies suggest these experiences can have profound and lasting effects on behaviors and attitudes. Among scholars, "mysticism" refers to a larger set of phenomena that can include visions, voices, and occult experiences, while "mystical experiences" or "mystical-type experiences" denotes a much narrower category.

Characterizing and Measuring Mystical-Type Experiences

Mystical experiences, according to the **philosopher Walter T. Stace**, are characterized by the experience of profound unity, expressed by the idea that "All is One"; the sense of that "One" as consciousness or a living presence; a sense that what is experienced is real; a deeply felt positive mood; the feeling of accessing the sacred or divine; paradoxicality; and a sense that the experience is difficult to put into words. Similar characteristics were identified by the American psychologist and philosopher William James in the early 1900s.

—psychedelics.berkeley.edu/religion-spirituality

OCD

For people with obsessive compulsive disorder (OCD), finding the right treatment can be difficult. While therapy and selective serotonin reuptake inhibitors (SSRIs) can help symptoms, that treatment does not work in up to 40% of people with OCD. But according to **survey results** published last week in *Nature Scientific Reports*, psychedelics might help people with OCD reduce their symptoms.
The study included 174 people with OCD symptoms who use psychoactive drugs. Eighty four percent of respondents reported using classic psychedelics including LSD and psilocybin. Of those, 66% reported that those classic psychedelic drugs were the most effective at reducing their OCD symptoms. Seventy two percent of the respondents reported using MDMA, but just 15% of those people said the drug worked to reduce their symptoms. "A higher proportion of participants chose classic psychedelics as the most efficient for OCD symptoms

when compared to other substances," the authors wrote. "The self-assessment of the therapeutic effect makes it prone to subjectivity bias, but a vast majority of classic psychedelics users, in our sample, *perceived* an improvement in their medical conditions following the intake of the substance."

—Hu, J. C. (2023, August 25). Self-administering psychedelics to treat OCD; California psychedelics bill on pause, Massachusetts ballot initiatives filed; and new guidelines for psychedelic practitioners. *The Microdose*. themicrodose.substack.com

Plus Therapy

The vast majority of research studies and regulated access models for psychedelics include not just administration of psychedelic drugs, but also some sort of therapy or guidance. In **a new article** published in *The American Journal of Psychiatry*, researchers at the University of Texas and psychedelics company COMPASS Pathways argue that the field needs to be clearer about the role of psychedelics and the role of therapy in treatment. "It is important to get this right, because regulatory bodies are asked to approve drugs with a defined efficacy and safety, not psychotherapies," they write.

They contend that psychedelic drugs like psilocybin and MDMA are driving therapeutic effects, and that preparation, in-session support, and integration are crucial for safety reasons but not for the efficacy of the drugs. "The effects observed thus far in the best controlled studies of psychedelic treatment must be attributed to the drug itself and not to psychotherapy," they write. "In the case of psilocybin, for example, let us say simply 'psilocybin treatment.'" A model of psychedelic treatment less tightly bound to a guided therapy approach might benefit psychedelics companies seeking to reduce costs — which might also in turn benefit some of the papers' authors, who are employed by, consult for, and have stock in several different psychedelics companies.

—Hu, J. C. (2023a, July 14). Does psilocybin treatment need therapy? Group files for a psychedelics ballot initiative in Massachusetts; A new

U.S. national poll asks respondents how they feel about psychedelics. *The Microdose.* themicrodose.substack.com

Acknowledgements

Writing a book takes a village as long as you let others in. Because I mostly write in solitude, the contents of these pages were a complete surprise to my family and friends, but they were with me the whole time even if they didn't know it! A special thank you goes to my partner, who let me hole up in my room, listen to the music on repeat, and burn a lot of candles that I shoved into a wine bottle for hours on end, just completely trusting the process of it all. I could have come out after that year with nothing but a blank page and you still would have cheered me on.

A huge thank you to my two wonderful children, you guys are the best cheerleaders!

Thank you to my dad, mom, and sister for loving me and being with me on this journey we call life. We will always have each other.

Thank you to my friends who saw me in these pages and being with me through all these stages of my life.

A bow of gratitude goes to Peggy who inspired much of this book. Thank you for always sitting and witnessing and loving. You hold us all in so many ways, thank you. And to her friends who shared their stories of the sacred medicine of psilocybin. I had a different book written, and then meeting with you changed the whole thing. Thank you for the medicine you gave me and that you have for so many years to so many others.

And finally, but absolutely not least, a huge heartfelt, and amazingly loud round of applause and confetti canon burst to my editor, Caitlin. Your love and enthusiasm for this book made me believe in myself again. Thank you for the time, the care, the diligence and intuitive approach you gave these pages. I am so glad we are also friends.

About the Author

B. Coil writes and paints in the corner of her bedroom in Austin, Texas where she lives with her partner and their two children. You can find her (sometimes) on IG here: @littleweirdwriter

B. COIL